THE JAM DOUGHNUT THAT RUINED MY LIFE

MARK LOWERY

Piccadilly
PRESS

First published in Great Britain in 2015 by
Piccadilly Press
Northburgh House, 10 Northburgh Street, London EC1V 0AT
www.piccadillypress.co.uk

A CIP catalogue record for this book is
available from the British Library.

ISBN: 978-1-84812-474-5

1 3 5 7 9 10 8 6 4 2

Typeset in Sabon 11/16 pt by
Palimpsest Book Production Limited, Falkirk, Stirlingshire

Printed and bound by Clays Ltd, St Ives Plc

Piccadilly Press is part of the Bonnier Publishing Group
www.bonnierpublishing.com

For S, J, S and O

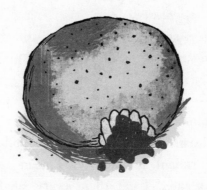

Hello. My name's Roman Garstang and my life was completely ruined . . . by a single jam doughnut.

Jam doughnuts only have two parts: jam. And doughnut. Oh, and a sprinkle of sugar on the top. They *should* be pretty easy to eat . . .

Instructions for Eating a Jam Doughnut

1. Bite into doughnut with front teeth. (If you have no front teeth, use your gums.)

2. Chew doughnut using back teeth. (If you have no back teeth, see Step 1.)

3. When doughnut becomes sloppy, swallow.

4. Repeat steps 1) to 3) until you have no more doughnut. (Note: Professional doughnut-eaters like me

always attempt to reach stage 4) without licking their lips. If you manage to do this, you may return to step 1) and enjoy a fresh doughnut.)

5.   Feel magnificent!

See? *Simple*.

Or at least it should've been, especially for me. I'm not brilliant at much but I'm an *expert* jam doughnut eater. I eat them every single day – morning snack, afternoon snack, after-school snack, after-snack snack . . . you get the picture. I must've eaten thousands of them. And until last week, the worst problems they'd ever given me were sticky fingers or a jammy chin.

It's no wonder I thought they were harmless.

But they're not harmless: they're **deadly**, like guns. Or sharks. Or sharks with guns.

Or trousers.

Yes, that's correct, *trousers*.

Every year in the UK, six thousand people are injured putting on their trousers. Can you believe that? *Six thousand!* Only a hundred people *in the whole world* are injured each year by sharks.

This means that trousers are way more dangerous than sharks. You wouldn't see a horror film about tracksuit bottoms terrorising a seaside town, though. And you wouldn't get lifeguards on beaches shouting: 'Everyone out of the water! Quick! There's a pair of man-eating jeans swimming round out there!'

Sometimes it's the everyday things that you think are the safest that cause the most damage.

MONDAY

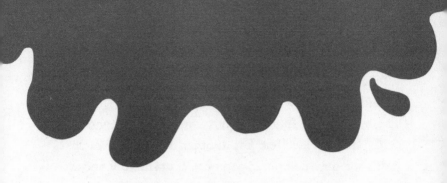

Morning

The Deadly Doughnut Causes Me to Headbutt a Sea Creature, Lose the Use of My Face and Half-drown my Girlfriend in Something Horrible

There's a reason why I know that trousers are more dangerous than sharks, and it's all because I was so worried the other night that I couldn't get to sleep.

My class, Year Six, have just finished our end of year tests. To celebrate this, our teacher Mrs McDonald organised a trip to an aquarium. Most people were excited but, as we got closer to it, I became more and more worried.

Normally my life is simple. I like it that way. I like how usually you can pick out any random day and you'll know what to expect. Up at seven-thirty. Go to school. Try to look busy. Stop for a doughnut. Go home. Have tea. Eat another doughnut. Watch TV or play computer games. Go upstairs. Choose underpants for the next day. Go to bed. Repeat.

Maybe this is why I love jam doughnuts so much. There are no nasty surprises – you know when you bite into one that sooner or later you're going to hit that delicious pool of sweet, sticky raspberry jam.

Unless of course you've picked up a lemon-flavoured one by mistake, that is. Lemon doughnuts are filled with this horrible yellow gloop called *curd* (personally I think a better name for it would be *crud*). They look perfectly nice from the outside – almost exactly the same as jam doughnuts, in fact – but inside they are pure, liquid evil.

Biting into a lemon doughnut by mistake is like waking up on Christmas morning, finding a BMX-shaped parcel at the end of your bed, tearing open the wrapping paper then finding out that, actually, you've been given a *model* of a BMX made entirely out of an old man's stinky toenail-cheese.

Disgusting.

Although I reckon the cheese from under an old man's toenails would taste slightly nicer than a lemon-flavoured doughnut.

Surprises can be bad news. So it's always better to know what's coming next. I didn't know what was going to happen on the aquarium trip and *that's* why I was worried about it. And two things were worrying me most of all:

1. **Pairs**. On school trips you have to pair up with a friend. I'm always stuck with this kid called Kevin Harrison who gets travel-sick. When we went to Skipton Castle, he barfed into my woolly hat (and I didn't realise until *after* I'd put it on, so I spent the rest of the trip combing chunks of half-digested Frosties out of my hair). Ever since then, Kevin's had the nickname 'The Vomcano'.

2. **The Shark Tunnel**. In one of the rooms at the aquarium, you walk through a massive shark tank. It's a tunnel made of glass, so the sharks swim right above your head. Darren Gamble reckons that sometimes they flood the tunnel and you've got to swim through instead. According to him, the aquarium 'loses about nine kids a year' but no one complains 'cos sharks is endangered, innit'.

I didn't really believe him (Gamble also claims that his grandma's got the longest neck in Europe and that he once found a live baby kangaroo inside an onion) but everyone had been going on about this flipping glass tunnel for weeks and I couldn't get it out of my head.

The night before the trip I had a nightmare about sitting next to a puking shark on the bus. I couldn't get back to sleep so I sneaked online, which is how I learned that sharks are actually much safer than trousers (there were no websites that said if they puke or not).

Afterwards I went back to bed feeling much more relaxed, but when I fell asleep I had *another* scary dream. In this one, Kevin Harrison's radioactive puke caused his trousers to come to life. I woke up just as they were trying to strangle me.

Because of this:

I finally got back to sleep at about four a.m., which meant . . .

I overslept till eight-thirty, which meant . . .

I didn't have time for breakfast.
Then, at the last minute . . .

I changed my trousers for a (much safer)
pair of shorts and swapped my planned undies
(grey briefs) for a pair of swimming trunks.
You know, just in case they did flood the tunnel.
As a result . . .

I was tired, hungry and very late when I got
to school. All of these things made me
uncomfortable: (especially the trunks, which
were a little bit too tight around my – you
know – **sensitive areas**).

No Eating on the Bus

By the time I flopped into my chair with my coat
and lunchbox, Mrs McDonald had already started
The Talk. The Talk happens before every school

trip. It goes like this: 'Blah blah . . . best behaviour . . . yakkety yak . . . representing the school . . . nyaaa nyaaa . . . no eating on the bus . . . etc.'.

Nobody seemed to be listening – apart from Jane Dixon, who is really clever and nice, and would never ignore a teacher. Most people were too excited about the trip to concentrate. Plus we were all in our own clothes (which makes you feel like you're not at school). PLUS Mrs McDonald was wearing *her* own clothes as well.

It's very strange, seeing a teacher in their out-of-school clothes – like seeing a spotty zebra or a soldier in a pink tutu. We're all used to seeing Mrs McDonald dressed in a standard teacher outfit: silk scarf, clumpy shoes, long dress that looks like a pair of old curtains, etc. I'm not trying to be nasty but today she looked like she'd just been dragged through the lost property bin. She was wearing outrageous green-and-purple leggings (even though she's about a thousand years old), the whitest trainers of all time, a first-aid-kit bumbag and a homemade knitted jumper with a massive picture of a guinea pig on the front.

In fact, the guinea pig looked more like a cow that'd been hit in the face with a frying pan. I only knew what it was because Mrs McDonald is *obsessed* with guinea pigs (or, as she sometimes calls them, 'piggywiggies').

She has a guinea pig calendar on the wall, with pictures of guinea pigs dressed up as Santa Claus (December), daffodils (March) and this month, a guinea pig doing a bungee jump. There's also a photo of her favourite guinea pig, Mr Wiggles, on her desk, surrounded by all the rosettes and cups he's won at guinea pig contests.

Mrs McDonald even looks a bit like a guinea pig herself. She has a stubby little snout, slightly sticky-out front teeth and great big cheeks (that may or may not be full of half-chewed carrots.

Anyway, while she told us to 'go now because the toilet on the bus is only for the driver', Kevin 'The Vomcano' Harrison waved at me from the other side of the table.

'Psst! Roman,' he whispered. 'Sit next to me on the way – I've got milkshake and a big bag of cola bottles!'

Hmm . . . I thought, pretending I hadn't heard him. *I think I'll give that a miss.*

I wasn't trying to be rude, by the way. Kevin's all right. Well, at least when he's not throwing up all over my stuff, that is. Still, I'm not great at maths but I'm pretty sure that:

milky drink + fizzy sweets + bus ride + sicky kid = AVOID

Despite this, the mention of food was enough to make my belly rumble. In my lunchbox there was a delicious Squidgy Splodge raspberry jam doughnut.

I imagined it sitting there next to my cheese sandwiches – the sugar stuck to the clingfilm; the dough all crispy on the outside and light and soft on the inside; the way the jam would ooze out as I lifted it towards my lips . . .

I could almost *hear* it calling to me. 'Ro-man!' it sang in a ghostly voice. 'You know you want to eat me, Roman. I'm sooo delicious, Roman . . . Are you listening to me, Roman?'

Funny, I thought, *the doughnut sounds just like Mrs McDonald.*

Mrs McDonald!

My eyes snapped open and I wiped the drool from my chin. Mrs McDonald was frowning at me.

'Yes, Mrs McDoughnut,' I said. 'I mean . . . Mrs McDonald.'

She tutted and shook her head, then carried on about how we were *definitely* not allowed to steal fish from the tanks.

I tried not to drift off again but I couldn't get the doughnut out of my head. *Should I take it out and eat it on the bus?* I thought.

I don't like to make decisions without thinking them through, so I considered it carefully for . . . *hmm* . . . about three milliseconds.

I *do* know that Mrs McDonald had just said that eating on the bus was against the rules. But *everyone* eats on the bus when they go on school trips. Seriously, when we went swimming the other week, Gamble ate an entire roasted chicken in less than twenty minutes. 'Don't eat on the bus' is just one of those things teachers say that they don't really mean, like, 'I've got eyes in the back of my head' or 'Maths is fun' or 'I was young once'.

Or at least, that's what I thought.

Trying not to let anyone see, I slid my coat over my lunchbox and opened it. Then I reached inside, slipped out the doughnut and put it into my pocket for the journey.

I didn't know it at the time, but this was the worst decision I'd ever made. This wasn't just any old raspberry jam doughnut. It was a doughnut that would ruin my life.

This was a deadly doughnut.

Ommmmm!

Almost immediately, Rosie Taylor (AKA Nosy Rosie) thrust her hand up in the air. '*Ommmmm*,' she said. 'I'm getting you done.'

Rosie Taylor sits next to me in class. I don't want to be horrible but she's got big, goggly frog-eyes and a small, mean mouth like a slug's bum. (OK, sorry, that *was* pretty horrible.) Both of these features are very handy for her hobbies, which are: 1) spying on people and 2) getting them into trouble.

The other thing about Rosie is that she absolutely *hates* me and always has done. I've never really understood why. I'm pretty quiet and I don't like to bother other people.

'Ssssh,' I said, 'please. I'm really hung–'

'Roman!' said Mrs McDonald sharply. Her big round cheeks started to turn red, which is a sign she's getting cross. 'That's twice. Sit next to me on the bus.'

This was terrible, but perhaps not as bad as sitting next to Kevin 'The Vomcano' Harrison. Every cloud has a silver lining, I guess. Rosie Taylor gave me a smarmy look then pulled out a little pocket mirror and began fiddling about with her hair (another of her annoying habits). She seemed delighted I was in trouble, even if it wasn't for the doughnut.

'Mrs McDonald, Mrs McDonald,' yelled Darren Gamble, leaping up and down and waving his arm about. 'Can I sit next to you too?'

I've mentioned Darren Gamble a few times. He's this strange, twitchy kid in my class with a funny little shaved head that makes him look like a baked bean. He only came to our school three weeks ago. According to him, he got expelled from St Joseph's for 'accidentally' setting fire to a nun. Seriously – a *nun*.

I don't know if that's true but he's always doing weird stuff like climbing on the school roof or eating worms. On his first day here he brought a dead magpie with him in his rucksack. Another time he had to go to hospital after sucking out the ink from an entire box of felt tips.

Most of my class find him funny but he gives me the collywobbles so I try to avoid him. I don't like people who are unpredictable. If my life's like a jam doughnut, his is like an explosion in a bakery.

Miss Clegg, Gamble's teaching assistant, looked up from the text message she was pretending not to send under the table. 'Good idea,' she said, rubbing her eyes. She always sounds like she's yawning.

I don't think Miss Clegg likes working with Gamble too much. I once heard her talking to another teaching assistant and she called Gamble 'that snot-nosed little turd', which wasn't very nice. Another time she broke wind in maths and then blamed it on him. This wound him up so much that he drank a whole bottle of Tipp-Ex.

I have to say I do feel a *bit* sorry for her. Until Gamble came along, Miss Clegg seemed to just float about the classes, doing the photocopying and stuff. Now she's got to spend all her time with him in case he tries to destroy the place. It must be one of the worst jobs ever, like washing a sumo wrestler's nappies or tasting cat food for a living.

'Mrs McDonald, I've got well-good music on my iPod,' said Gamble. 'We can share earphones, miss. All my favourite bands are on there – Hedgehog Bloodbath, The Kitten Slicers, Cheese Grater for Your Eyeballs. I've even got the new album by

Sweaty Steve and The Exploding Grandmas. It's totally banging, miss, you'll love it.'

'Darren. I think I've told you before that I don't really *like* heavy metal music,' said Mrs McDonald. 'You'll be with Miss Clegg.'

Miss Clegg went back to texting. 'Great. Stuck with *him* all day,' I heard her mutter.

'Awwww,' Gamble moaned. 'Can't I sit on your lap, Mrs McDonald? You're my most favouritest teacher ever.'

I'm not sure why, but for some reason Gamble *loves* Mrs McDonald. On his first day he latched on to her like a verruca and she hasn't been able to get rid of him since.

'Did you take your tablets this morning, Darren?' Mrs McDonald asked.

Everyone giggled.

'No, miss,' said Gamble, bouncing up and down in his chair. 'I gave 'em to the dog.'

Mrs McDonald closed her eyes and pinched the bridge of her nose. 'That sounds like animal cruelty to me –'

Gamble held up his hand to stop her. 'Don't worry, miss. It's for his own good. This week he's been a bit bitey.'

'"Bitey"?' she asked.

'Yeah,' said Gamble. 'He always gets like that when he's got worms up his bum.'

Most of the class laughed. Mrs McDonald slapped her hand to her forehead. Kevin 'The Vomcano' Harrison took deep breaths like he was going to throw up.

Gamble grinned. 'My uncle's the same when *he* gets worms up–'

'Thank you, Darren,' interrupted Mrs McDonald. 'You and Miss Clegg had better sit behind me. This is going to be *fun*.'

O-M-G!

The drive to the aquarium was definitely *not* fun. For a start I couldn't sneak even a nibble of my doughnut while I was sat next to Mrs McDonald. She kept pointing out of the window and saying teacher-y things like 'Those clouds are called *cumulus* – don't you think they look like fluffy, flying guinea pigs?'

I shrugged and said nothing. They looked like clouds to me.

On top of this, Kevin 'The Vomcano' Harrison

erupted before we'd even left the car park and spent the whole journey with his head in a bucket. He was across the aisle from me in the puker's seat (you know, the one they reserve at the front of the bus so the travel-sick kids can see out of the windscreen). It smelled *awful* – like old yoghurt mixed with satsumas. He kept turning to me between spews and saying things like, 'Roman, I think there's a cola bottle stuck in the back of my nose' and 'Urgh – it's definitely getting milkier with every heave'. It was horrible but at least it killed my appetite for a while.

And even worse, all the way to the aquarium, Gamble was shaking my chair violently and patting me on the head and pinching my ear. And he just kept . . . on . . . talking. Constantly. 'Rosie Taylor's telling everyone you've got a doughnut in your pocket can I have some doughnut Mrs McDonald make him give me some doughnut . . .'

Whenever Gamble's being annoying, Mrs McDonald and Miss Clegg try to ignore him. I think they expect him to get bored after a while but he never does. He's like a hyperactive wasp in a tin. At least the teachers also ignored what he was saying about the doughnut in my trousers. Even so, I knew

I had to eat it soon. It was leaking jam into my pocket.

I was relieved when we reached the aquarium and I could finally escape. Straight away we had to line up in our pairs. I was worried about who I'd end up with but Mrs McDonald said she'd be Kevin 'The Vomcano' Harrison's partner 'just in case' and Gamble should stick with Miss Clegg. When she heard this, Miss Clegg looked up in the sky and said, 'Oh, you are *kidding* me.' She isn't very good at hiding her feelings.

I was left alone. *Lovely stuff,* I thought. *I'll wait till it's quiet and eat my doughnut then.*

I'd just joined the back of the line when I felt a tap on my shoulder. 'Would you like to be my partner?' said a voice.

I turned around and *hot potato!* It was Jane Dixon. I nearly coughed up a lung.

Earlier I said I don't like surprises. This is because most surprises are terrible e.g. the spider in your bed, the drawing pin on your chair, the sudden attack by your trousers, etc. However, this surprise was completely different.

As I sort of mentioned before, Jane Dixon is:

1. **Brainy**. She sits at the clever table for everything and always has her work up on the board.
2. **Well-behaved**. She's on the school council and she gets merits and certificates all the time.
3. **Nice**. She does loads of jobs for teachers and helps the little kids when they bump their knees in the playground.

Well, what I didn't mention is that she's also, you know . . . ahem – *nice*, if you know what I mean. She has a nice head and a nice face. Her hair is nice too, like a brown waterfall. But not brown because the water's dirty – I mean brown like hot chocolate. And she smells nice too, like strawberry-flavoured washing powder. Oh, and the best thing about Jane? Her initials are JD – just like my favourite snack.

Jane never normally talks to me. She's like a beautiful golden doughnut in a glass case – something that looks amazing but is painfully out of reach.

'Well . . . I . . . er . . .' I spluttered.

'O-M-G!' announced Rosie Taylor. She always says things like O-M-G and L-O-L. She thinks they make her sound cool and grown up. I disagree. 'Roman and Jane are boyfriend and girlfriend!'

The rest of the class gasped but Jane Dixon calmly turned to Rosie and said five incredible words: 'So what if we are?'

O-M-G!

The Dark Zone

Jane's question was too much for our classmates. They all suddenly went mental, leaping up and down like frenzied monkeys.

Rosie Taylor put her hands on her hips. 'I'd never have put you two together, Jane. Roman's so . . .' she looked me up and down, '*disgusting* and . . . *weird.*'

'I'm standing right here,' I said.

Even though I've never understood why, Rosie is *always* nasty to me. E.g. last week she told Mrs McDonald that I'd hidden the school goldfish in my underpants (it turned out that Gamble had eaten it). In Year Five, for some reason, she spread a rumour that I had 'eight nipples, like a cat'.

Still, just because I'm used to her being horrible all the time, it doesn't mean I *like* it.

'Well,' said Jane coolly, 'I think Roman's got *lots* of good things going for him. Plus he's *totally* cute.'

I felt myself going red. No one had ever called me *totally cute* before. Apart from Mum, who says I've got 'big brown eyes like a baby camel, hair like a poodle and a face like a sweet angel'. I'm not trying to boast, by the way. I know all mums say that sort of stuff, even if their kids look like swamp monsters.

'Whatevs,' said Rosie, pouting and showing Jane the palm of her hand. She turned to the rest of the line and swept her hair back dramatically. 'It's official, people. We'll have to call them Joman. Or Romane. They're an item now.'

'Yes, we are,' said Jane to no one in particular. I have to say, she looked extremely pleased with herself.

'Yuck,' said Rosie. 'Pass me the sick bucket, Kevin.'

I gulped. I mean, being Jane's boyfriend was pretty epic news but still, it would've been nice to have had some warning so I could prepare myself.

'*Ahem*,' I said to Jane. 'Just so I know . . . what *exactly* do I have to do?'

Jane patted my head. 'Don't worry. We don't have to *kiss* each other or anything.'

'Phew,' I said. Don't get me wrong, she didn't *look* like she was carrying any diseases but still – if putting on trousers can kill you, imagine what kissing a girl could do.

'We'll just walk around together and stuff,' she said, twirling her hair around her finger. 'Fish are *so* romantic.'

I had no idea if this was true or not but I needed to say something boyfriendly. *Er . . . how about a quick joke?* I thought.

I cleared my throat. 'Well, in that case,' I said, 'I'll send you a tin of tuna on Valentine's Day.'

Jane laughed. 'You're so *funny,* Roman!'

Yes! It turned out I was brilliant at being a boyfriend.

'But of course you won't send me a tin of tuna,' she said, her face suddenly turning serious. 'You'll send me a nice card and a teddy bear and you'll write me a poem as well, because that's what boyfriends do.'

'Oh,' I said, my palms beginning to sweat. That was a lot to remember. I wished I'd brought a pad with me to jot it all down. Maybe being a boyfriend wasn't quite as easy or fun as it looked. 'Er . . . OK.'

She wrinkled her nose up at me. 'You're so sweet.'

The entrance to the aquarium was shaped like a shark's open mouth. I knew how harmless sharks are so I thought this was pretty cool. Jane didn't. 'Oh, Roman,' she said, gripping my arm. 'I'm *sooo* scared of sharks.'

This was officially the first time that a girl had ever held my arm. I wasn't sure what to do so I decided to make her feel better using a fact.

'Actually you should be more scared of your own trousers,' I said.

Jane unhooked her arm from mine and looked at me strangely. There was a long, uncomfortable silence, which was only broken when Gamble suddenly clambered up on top of the entrance and rode the shark's nose like a horse, screeching, 'Yee-ha! Ride 'em, sharkboy!'

When Miss Clegg eventually pulled him down by the ankle, we trooped into the foyer. Mrs McDonald handed everyone a clipboard and told us to take notes and draw pictures of anything interesting. Gamble bashed each of us on the head with his as we walked past.

The first room we went into was called 'The Dark Zone'. It was pitch black, with dimly lit tanks full of strange-looking deep-sea fish. There were loads of mums and toddlers in there, and the kids were all running about screaming.

Dark and noisy, I thought, *the perfect place to eat my doughnut.*

As the rest of the class dodged past the little ones to huddle round the tanks, I hung back. I reached into my pocket . . .

There was a tap on my shoulder.

'Hi, Roman,' whispered Jane into my ear. 'I wondered where you'd gone.'

'Oh. Er. Hi,' I said, quickly pulling my hand out.

'So . . . Rosie mentioned something on the bus,' said Jane. 'Something about . . . I don't know, a jam doughnut, or something?'

'I'm not sure what you mean,' I lied. I didn't want the whole world to know about it.

'And I just thought,' said Jane, like she hadn't heard me, 'that since you're such an amazing boyfriend . . . you might just let me have a tiny nibble.'

In the green light from the tanks, her eyes twinkled like Jelly Tots on a birthday cake. I did my best to say no to her. 'But, I'm *really* hungry,' I said, 'and I haven't had any breakfast.'

Jane suddenly looked really sad. 'My mum and dad don't let me have anything sweet at home,' she said, wiping something out of her eye. 'And I don't get pocket money so I never get the chance to buy a doughnut for myself. You'll share an incey bit with me, won't you, Romy-womy? Pwetty pwease.'

I didn't know what to do. I felt sorry for her – imagine a life without doughnuts! What would you have to live for? – but still, this wasn't just any old cake she was asking for.

A horrible thought came into my head. 'You're not just going out with me for my doughnut, are you?' I said.

Jane's eyes opened wide. 'Absolutely not!'

She said it so loudly that half the class turned around. 'Check it out, peeps. Looks like Joman's relationship is on the rocks,' grinned Rosie. A few people sniggered before turning back to the tanks.

'I've always liked you,' continued Jane, looking at her shoes. 'It's just a total coincidence that on the day you become my boyfriend you just happen to have a delicious jam doughnut in your pocket.'

She smiled at me.

I didn't know whether or not to believe her. 'Well . . .'

Thankfully I was interrupted by Mrs McDonald screaming: 'Get out of there!'

Everything Starts to Go Wrong

Darren Gamble was *inside* one of the tanks! He was holding his breath and doing breaststroke from one side to the other. People were slapping the green, scummy glass and laughing and cheering.

It took me a moment to realise there wasn't actually any water in the tank. There was a big sign outside that read: 'Jellyfish Moved – Cleaning in Progress'. But even by his standards this was pretty nuts and I didn't like it at all.

When they'd managed to get him out (there was a door behind the tank that some idiot had left unlocked), Mrs McDonald asked Miss Clegg to hold Gamble's hand. Miss Clegg put on a glove, as though Gamble's hand was covered in toxic waste. Knowing Gamble, this wasn't completely impossible.

'Right. Next room!' said Mrs McDonald, herding us out. Her cheeks were now the same colour as a fire engine.

Halfway along a bright corridor, everyone suddenly stopped. A little girl about three years old was sitting on her potty right in front of us and wailing, 'Wee-wee not come! Wee-wee not come!'

'Cool,' said Gamble.

'OK, darling,' said her mum, trying to sound calm but not really doing a very good job. 'I told you this wasn't a good potty place. Let's try somewhere else.'

'NOOO!' screamed the girl, clamping her hands round the potty. 'Wee-wee right here!'

The mum bit her lip and looked at Mrs McDonald.

'Don't worry, we've all been there,' joked Mrs McDonald. By this, I hope she meant that she'd been the parent of a small child. The idea of Mrs McDonald using a potty was not something I wanted to think about. 'Stay left, everyone.'

We walked in line past the potty and into the next room, which was called 'Shallow Hall'. It was much lighter than The Dark Zone; it would be way harder to eat my doughnut in there.

Inside the hall were two large, shallow pools that you could lean over the side of. In one, there was a selection of rays and crabs. The other one had a big sign on it that read:

DANGER!
POISONOUS JELLYFISH!
KEEP HANDS OUT!

I guessed this was where they'd been moved to from the empty tank in the other room.

While the class began drawing the rays, Gamble leaned right over and shoved his head under the water then shook it all off like a wet dog.

'Shall we have our doughnut now?' said Jane, smiling sweetly at me.

Our doughnut? Good grief. Since when had it become *our* doughnut? I didn't like the sound of this at all.

'I'm not sure,' I said, uneasily.

Jane's bottom lip began to wobble.

'All right, all right,' I said. The last thing I wanted to do was upset her. We hadn't even had our ten-minute anniversary yet.

I looked over to Mrs McDonald. She had turned away from everyone and was talking on her mobile phone. By the sound of things she wasn't happy – I caught the odd phrase like: 'Yes, you buffoon – I *know* he's put on weight. What do I pay you for . . .?'

I don't think teachers are allowed to chat on their mobile phones when they're meant to be looking after children but this was *brilliant*. She was totally distracted. I had to grab my chance.

I reached into my pocket and carefully pulled out the jam doughnut. Peeling off the clingfilm and covering it with my clipboard, I broke off a tiny bit and placed it into Jane's hand. This made me feel like a total hero – like I'd just given her one of my kidneys or something. Yep, I was a *terrific* boyfriend.

Jane looked at it for a moment. *Nice one, Roman,* I thought. *She's so delighted that she's speechless.*

'Pretty awesome, eh?' I said, cheerfully, 'Don't eat it all at once.'

She slowly raised her eyes to mine. 'A sweaty little crumb?' she hissed. 'Is that all I'm worth to you?'

'But . . . but . . . but . . .' I said, totally surprised. 'What's wrong with it?'

She held it up to my face. 'Firstly, you'd need a microscope to see it,' she said. 'And secondly . . . it's *warm*.'

I hunched my shoulders. 'I'm sorry. It's been in my pocket for an hour.'

'Are you trying to . . . make me sad?' she said, her voice cracking and her face crumpling up. 'I thought you were kind.'

This was terrible. I thought she'd be delighted but she was *weeping*. People were staring at us. I needed to do something fast. Desperately, I split the whole thing in two and, as jam oozed out onto my fingers, I handed her half.

Well, OK, quite a bit less than half.

Jane brightened up immediately. 'Thanks, Roman,' she chirped.

'Hang on,' I said, 'Were you . . . *pretending* to cr–'

Before I could finish, Jane dived in suddenly and kissed me on the cheek. This wasn't actually as bad as I'd feared. In fact, it was pretty ace. I let out a noise that sounded a bit like: *Mneeep.*

'This is *so* romantic!' she said.

The romantic mood was rather spoiled by the little girl crying from the corridor: 'Wee-wee come soon. Wee-wee come soon!'

'Cover me,' said Jane, bending her head down to eat the doughnut.

I stood in front of her and tried to look on the bright side. I'd lost almost half a doughnut to Jane Dixon but she *was* my girlfriend and she *was* nice. Maybe it wasn't so bad after all. Maybe after this she'd get hold of some money and start buying them for *me*. Maybe she'd bring me a whole box of doughnuts every single day! *Yes!* That would be brilliant.

And then everything started to go wrong.

'Gizza bit,' said Gamble, suddenly appearing behind me.

I quickly turned round, holding my half-doughnut behind my back.

'No,' said Jane, doing the same. She hadn't quite managed to get it into her mouth. 'He's my boyfriend so he only shares with me.'

'Shut it, melon-head,' said Gamble. His face and hair were still soaked.

Jane turned to me. She was fuming. 'Are you going to let him speak to me like that?'

'Er . . . I . . .'

Nobody had told me that being a boyfriend meant having to stand up to nutters. I don't want to sound like a wimp, but come on! We *are* talking about a kid who once bit a duck in the playground.

'Come on, why're you being so horrible? I just wanna bit of doughnut, innit,' said Gamble, shaking me by the shoulders.

Thankfully, Miss Clegg stepped in for a change. 'Darren,' she called in her bored voice, 'come and draw this flat thing over here, whatever it is.'

''S'all right, you can save it me for later,' said Gamble, before bouncing off.

Wonderful.

'Don't be scared of him,' said Jane. 'If you're not having it, I will.'

Well, that sealed it. She might've been my girlfriend but there was no way Jane was getting the whole thing. In any case, maybe he'd forget; Gamble has a terrible memory. On Friday he forgot to put on his trousers after PE and accidentally went out to play in his undies.

Actually, knowing Gamble, this might not have been an accident.

I peered over the barrier into the stingray tank. Then I took the rest of the doughnut in my cupped hand and, pretending to cough, lifted it up to my open mou–

THWAP!

Something cold and wet smashed me in the face.

A Massive Blob

For a moment I just stood there, stunned. Then my cheeks began to sting. I looked down at the floor. Lying by my feet was what looked like a massive blob of blackcurrant jelly.

Oh dear, I thought. *JELLY!*

As in jelly . . . *fish*.

Wonderful.

I told you that most surprises were bad. And being smashed in the chops with a flying jellyfish is probably about the worst one I've ever had. The throbbing pain in my face rapidly got worse.

'What the piggy-wig happened here?' said Mrs McDonald, ending her phone call and striding towards me.

Gamble ran over too. His clipboard was soaking wet, like he'd just, ooh, I don't know, used it to fling a poisonous sea creature at my head, perhaps?

'You'll never believe it, Mrs McDonald,' he said, 'but Roman was eating a jam doughnut and the jellyfish saw him and it just *leapt* out of the tank and *smacked* him right in the face.'

Mrs McDonald squinted at him. 'Pardon?'

'I fink Dawen fwew it at be,' I said, but my lips were turning numb and I couldn't speak properly.

'As if I would?' said Gamble, narrowing his eyes at me. 'If you hadn't tried to eat the doughnut, this wouldn't have happened.'

'Miss Clegg?' said Mrs McDonald. 'Did Darren do this?'

'Didn't see anything,' said Miss Clegg, looking up from her mobile.

Excellent.

'Innocent till proven guilty,' said Gamble. 'That's what my uncle always says.'

'So,' said Mrs McDonald, 'I'm supposed to believe that this jellyfish just *hurled itself* out of the water and *attacked* Roman.'

'Yes, it's true,' said Rosie Taylor, looking smug as she picked up my now soggy half-doughnut from the floor. 'Look what I found. Hashtag: "Caught red-handed".'

Mrs McDonald raised an eyebrow at me. 'So it was all your fault, Roman?'

'No -iss,' I moaned. 'Ask 'ane,'

My girlfriend would explain everything. She'd tell Mrs McDonald that Gamble threw the jellyfish. Maybe she'd even pretend I had nothing to do with the doughnut.

Mrs McDonald turned to her. 'Jane, don't tell me you were involved in this too? I am surprised.'

Jane's cheeks looked ready to burst and her mouth was clamped shut. She chewed rapidly, shaking her head. Then she swallowed hard before saying, 'No,

I wasn't, Mrs McDonald. I tried to make him stop eating but . . . it was too late . . .'

She burst into tears.

Thanks, *girlfriend*.

By now my face felt like it was being slowly inflated with burning hot air. Gamble carried the jellyfish on his clipboard back to its tank and tipped it in.

'I warned you about eating,' sighed Mrs McDonald, before clapping her hands together. 'Right. Medical emergency. Rosie – run to reception and get them to call an ambulance. Roman – don't move.'

Rosie smiled cruelly. 'Should I call the funeral parlour as well, miss? You know . . . just in case?'

I started to feel sick.

'Just hurry along,' said Mrs McDonald, as Rosie ran off laughing. 'The rest of you, line up.'

The class reacted like they'd just been told the world was about to end: 'But what about the shark tunnel?' said someone.

'Roman headbutts a fish and we all miss out.'

'Thanks a lot, dinghy lips.'

'Borry,' I said, struggling to speak. 'Bu' I'm in a 'ot o' pain 'ere.'

Nobody seemed bothered that I'd just been attacked

by a deadly sea creature. What if my skin melted? What if my face dropped off? Did anybody actually care?

Well, yes, someone did care.

Sadly that someone was Darren Gamble.

'Mrs McDonald,' said Gamble, tugging on her sleeve.

'What now?' said Mrs McDonald.

'Wee, miss.'

'*Wee?*'

I didn't like the sound of this.

Gamble flashed a big grin at her. 'Wee cures jellyfish stings. We should all wee on him. Come on, everyone. Wee on Roman.'

A few people actually nodded as though this was a good idea.

'I've heard that,' said Miss Clegg.

'Darren!' barked Mrs McDonald. 'Pull up your flies. If anyone's going to wee on this boy, it's going to be a trained doctor.'

I didn't see how this was much better.

Suddenly Gamble's face lit up and he ducked out of the room.

'Come back . . . or whatever . . .' said Miss Clegg half-heartedly.

After a few moments, Gamble returned with something in his hands.

This *really* wasn't good. I shook my head violently and tried to beg him not to do it but all that came out was: 'Hnuffa hnuffa hnuffa.'

'Now, now, Darren,' said Mrs McDonald. 'Put that down.'

Gamble was holding a potty full of yellow liquid.

'Hey! Give that back!' cried the mum from the corridor, storming into the room. Behind her I could hear the little girl crying.

Predictably, Gamble didn't listen.

'It's for your own good,' he said, hurling the contents of the potty right at me.

Fortunately I ducked out of the way just in time.

*Un*fortunately Jane was still standing right behind me.

Chaos

All in all, you could say that Jane took the faceful of warm toddler-wee quite well.

Well, you *could* say that. But only if by 'quite well' you mean that she started screaming and completely freaking out. Kevin Harrison was so disturbed that he threw up into the stingray pool.

'Ooh, yuck. That's disgusting and it's all Roman's fault,' said Rosie Taylor, who'd just returned to the room. 'The manager's on his way, Mrs McDonald. Maybe we can ask him to call the police so Roman gets put in jail.'

'Cool! It's like an oil slick,' said Gamble. 'Except it's an oil *sick!* Geddit?'

To emphasise this 'joke' he punched me hard in the arm. 'Ow! Sno fu-ee,' I said.

'Hope no one expects me to clear that up,' yawned Miss Clegg.

While this was happening, Mrs McDonald was being yelled at by the mum of the toddler. And the little girl, who'd now got her potty back, was dancing round the room with it on her head. It was chaos.

In the end the manager came and our class was asked to leave. Miss Clegg took everyone to the bus while I went to the first aid room to wait for an ambulance with Mrs McDonald.

When the paramedic turned up she scraped and wiped my swollen face to get rid of the poison. Then she spread some cream across the worst bits and gave me an ice pack. 'Bit puffy but no real damage,' she said. 'You'll be fine with some painkillers. Get your mum to take you to A&E if the swelling doesn't go down.'

'Phew! I was frightened his head was going to burst,' said Mrs McDonald. 'Imagine the forms I'd have to fill in.'

Thanks a bunch. Nice to know you care.

'You're a lucky lad,' said the paramedic.

Lucky? I'd just been hit with a flying jellyfish when all I wanted was a jam doughnut. I hadn't exactly got five numbers and the bonus ball.

'I wouldn't eat anything for the rest of the day, though,' said the paramedic, zipping up her bag. 'Just in case you feel ill.'

My stomach did a back-flip. *No food until tomorrow?* I was already absolutely starving. And, worst of all, no food would mean no jam doughnuts. I didn't usually go that long without one. What would happen to me? I could get sick, or come out in a rash, or my head could fall off. This wasn't good.

By the time Mum arrived to take me home, the rest of the class had been sitting in the bus for almost an hour and they weren't too happy. When I got on with Mrs McDonald to collect my lunchbox and coat, Gamble and a few others stood up and booed like the whole thing was my fault. Miss Clegg even joined in, which I thought was pretty low.

I tried to speak to Jane but she just turned away and looked out of the window. My face still burning, I dragged my feet off the bus and Mum drove me home.

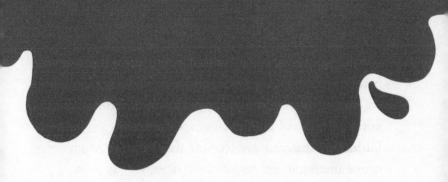

Evening

The Deadly Doughnut Triggers an Unwelcome Visit and I Have to Watch Something Disgusting

I spent the afternoon in my bedroom. My eyelids were swollen and sore so I couldn't play on the computer or watch TV or read; I just had to lie there with my massive moon-head, doing nothing.

I must've drifted off to sleep for a few hours because when I looked at my alarm clock it was suddenly half-past four. Nearly teatime. I called down to Mum to ask for a drink but she didn't reply so I put on my dressing gown and went downstairs.

It was now more than six hours since I'd tried

to eat that surprisingly dangerous jam doughnut. Half of it was in the bin at the aquarium. The other half was in Jane's stomach. I was pretty sure that nothing else bad could come from it.

I was wrong.

The deadly doughnut had set wheels in motion, wheels of doughnut-fuelled disaster and destruction . . .

I paused at the door to the front room. There was laughter coming from inside. Dad wouldn't be home yet. Maybe Mum was on the phone to Auntie Kath. I shrugged, opened the door and instantly wished I hadn't. If my eyes hadn't been two tiny slits, I reckon they would've popped out of my head.

'Hello, sleepy,' said Mum. 'Glad you've finally woken up for your visitor.'

'Hi, Roman,' said Jane, who was sitting on the sofa right next to my mum. 'Nice PJs.'

Quick as I could, I pulled my dressing gown closed. I was wearing my Postman Pat pyjamas, which are at least five years old, maybe more. They finish about halfway up my arms, legs and belly and they're stained here and there with splodges of old, crusty breakfast. They're totally comfortable but probably not what you'd choose to wear in front of your girlfriend.

'What are you doing here?' I asked. At least my voice had returned to normal, even if my head felt like an over-inflated spacehopper.

'That's not very polite, Roman,' said Mum, standing up. 'Jane came round to see if you're OK. I tried to wake you but you were sleeping like a dead sloth.'

I guess Mum was a little bit right. It wasn't very polite of me, but still – Jane had let me get into trouble *and* ignored me on the bus.

'I also came round to say sorry,' said Jane, quickly. 'I panicked a bit when Mrs McDonald asked about the doughnut. I've never been in trouble before. And when you got on the bus, I didn't want you to see me with that . . . *stuff* in my hair. I've had a wash now, though.'

She smiled at me. She was wearing a dolphin t-shirt. I guessed she'd bought it from the gift shop at the aquarium while I was with the paramedic. I felt bad – her other top must've been soaked. And she was my *girlfriend*, after all. 'Well, ahem, I'm sorry too. I shouldn't have ducked.'

'We're quits then,' she said, making her nose go all wrinkly like a Walnut Whip. 'How's your face?'

'Bit better,' I said. 'It only hurts when I breathe.'

Jane laughed. 'Your mum's just showing me pictures of you when you were a baby.'

Oh come on, I thought, *not in front of my girlfriend.*

I should probably explain a few things about my mum here. She's pretty much the most embarrassing person of all time. I'm an only child so she takes photos of everything I do. Literally. You name it and there's a photo of me doing it: brushing my teeth, eating soup, putting on my socks, combing my hair. Then she shows them to anyone who's in the house for more than about three seconds.

Jane pointed to the photo album that was open on the sofa. 'I particularly like this one of you in the bath.'

I dived forward and flicked the album shut. 'That's enough of that.'

'He's so grouchy when he wakes up,' said Mum. 'Humpty *Grump*ty we call him.'

I took a deep breath.

'Rosie Taylor said you might need to have your head amputated,' Jane told me.

'Huh,' I said. 'Typical.'

'Why would she say such a nasty thing about your lovely little noggin?' said Mum, ruffling my hair.

I ducked out of the way. 'She doesn't like me much, Mum.'

'When you were at nursery, Rosie was your best friend,' Mum said, sounding surprised. 'In fact, me and her mum used to joke that you two would get married.'

'Please stop,' I said. Of all the embarrassing things Mum has ever said, this was surely the worst.

Mum didn't seem to hear to me. 'Here, look at this . . .'

She flipped through the photo album, stopping at a picture of me and Rosie, aged about three. We were . . . *hugging* each other. Hugging Rosie Taylor, I tell you! Yuck! I'd rather hug a camel with chickenpox.

'Hmm,' I said. 'Maybe we could burn that one.'

'Aw . . . I think it's sweet,' said Jane.

'Then, well, there was this . . . *incident* that happened. Rosie and her mum cut us off after that and . . .' Mum's voice trailed away.

'She's been awful to me every single day since,' I said, finishing the sentence for her. I'd no idea what the 'incident' was but it was probably absolutely nothing. Rosie has never needed much of an excuse to be horrible to me.

'Anyway,' said Mum to Jane, 'lovely to finally see Roman have a friend over. Can I get you anything from the kitchen?'

'I'll have a doughn–' I began but Mum interrupted me.

'Sorry, dumpling, I was just talking to Jane. You're not allowed food, remember?'

My stomach rumbled. I'd hoped that she wouldn't find out about that rule but Mrs McDonald had told her at the aquarium.

'Well,' said Jane, licking her lips, 'since Roman mentioned it, *I* wouldn't mind a doughnut, please.'

I gulped.

A Complete Pig

Mum came back in with some plates and a cardboard box of doughnuts.

'Oooh, this looks nice,' said Jane, reading from the box. '"Squidgy Splodge Doughnuts – By Appointment to the Royal Family" it says here. Very posh!'

'Roman only likes the best doughnuts. I have to get these out of the special cabinet in the cake aisle. He has a screaming fit if I buy the own-brand ones,' trilled Mum. 'Don't you, my little prince?'

Screaming fit. My little prince. Could this day get any worse?

'And don't ask me about what he did when I bought a lemon-flavoured one by mistake,' said Mum, as Jane examined the box and licked her lips.

I ground my teeth together. Doughnuts are like people. There are lots of different types. Some are amazing. Some are just OK. Some are disgusting. Lemon-flavoured doughnuts are definitely disgusting. Only a complete idiot would like them. Imagine biting into a doughnut expecting delicious raspberry jam and getting a mouthful of sour lemon curd instead. *Yuck.* The raspberry jam's the best bit. Liking the lemon ones is the same as saying, 'I love watching football. But only when there's no ball. And no players. And no pitch.'

'Hey look,' said Mum, pointing at the box. 'There's a competition. You can win a year's supply of doughnuts. All you have to do is text that number and –'

'You know what,' said Jane, suddenly, 'I wonder what the doughnuts taste like. Shall we just, you know. . .?' Her voice tailed off and she nodded towards the box.

I tried to raise an eyebrow but my face was still too sore and swollen.

'Oh . . . of course,' said Mum, 'where are my manners? I'll pop one on a plate and . . .'

'Oh, you can put all of them on a plate if you like,' said Jane, laughing a bit *too* hard.

'I like a girl with a good appetite,' said Mum, smiling. She looked surprised, though, as she opened the box. 'Oh. There's only one left. How did that happen?'

I scratched the back of my head and tried to look innocent. 'No idea. Maybe a cat got in or something . . .'

'Oh well,' said Mum. 'Now they are quite big. Should I cut it in half?'

Jane ran her hand through her hair. 'I think I could manage a whole one, please.'

A whole one? I thought. *What am I going to eat tomorrow?!* Blood rushed to my face, making it tingle.

Mum cleared her throat. 'Well. I thought I might save a bit for when Roman's allowed –'

'Roman won't mind,' smiled Jane. 'Will you, Roman?'

'Well, I will kind of mind . . . a bit,' I said.

'Manners, Roman. Of course you won't,' said

Mum, placing the lone doughnut onto a plate. It was horrible to watch – like she was giving away one of my legs.

Mum handed Jane the plate. 'Enjoy.'

'Oh, I will,' said Jane, licking her lips.

'I'll leave you two lovebirds to it,' smiled Mum, edging out of the room.

Lovebirds? I told you she's embarrassing. I felt like diving out of the window. After about five seconds, I finally plucked up the courage to look at Jane. Amazingly, she didn't seem to have noticed what Mum had said.

She was holding up the plate in her hands, turning it round and studying the doughnut as if it was a precious jewel. She sniffed it and held her breath for a good five seconds. 'Mmm – exquisite.'

'Are you really going to eat the whole thing?' I asked but I might as well have been speaking to a turnip – Jane was completely hypnotised by the doughnut. I'd never seen her like this before. It was like she'd been waiting her whole life for this moment.

Her tongue flicked out like a snake's. 'Come to Momma,' she whispered, lifting the doughnut up to her mouth.

You know at the beginning when I explained how

to eat a doughnut? Simple, wasn't it? You'd think most people would be able to follow those instructions without any hassle. Well, not Jane. Maybe it was because she'd not had many opportunities to eat one before. Or maybe she'd always had to eat them in private so she'd never learned the correct way to do it.

The reason is not important. All that matters is that what she did next was utterly disgusting.

First Jane squashed the doughnut flat and licked up the splodge of jam that oozed out onto her fingers from the hole at the side. However it got *much* worse when . . .

. . . she scraped the sugary coating off the top with her teeth, then. . .

. . . yanked off a clump of dough and. . .

. . . sucked on it before. . .

. . . squishing it into a soggy ball. . .

. . . and tossing it into her gob.

I looked on in horror as she shoved the rest of the doughnut into her mouth and savaged it like a bloodthirsty hyena. She was making all these *mmmnaym-mmmnaym* noises and smacking her lips together.

My girlfriend was a complete pig.

This was a terrible surprise, like finding a frog in a can of lemonade, or buying a cool pair of trousers then learning that they want to murder you.

Jane swallowed hard, let out a little burp then giggled and put her hand over her mouth. It had taken her about eight seconds to demolish the whole thing.

'Thanks, Roman,' she grinned, displaying lumps of chewed-up dough between her teeth. 'You can definitely get me more of that . . . *boyfriend*.'

For the second time that day Jane leaned in and

pecked me on the cheek. I got goosebumps up my arms – but not in a good way. They were more like the kind of goosebumps you might get when a rat runs over your foot.

I wiped my face.

'Right. Gotta go,' she said. 'Mum and Dad think I'm at Rosie's house.'

She'd *lied* to her parents! That wasn't like Jane, was it? The doughnut had turned her into a pig *and* a liar.

'Anyone'd think you only came over for the doughnut,' I said, trying my best to sound jokey.

'Of course not,' Jane laughed. 'Don't be silly. As if? What a thing to say.' There was a bit of a pause. 'Are you sure there aren't any more?'

'No,' I said. This was not true. There's always an emergency doughnut in a plastic box in the cupboard. I'm not meant to know about it; Mum keeps the emergency doughnut for her and Dad in case I eat them all. There was no way Jane was going to guzzle that as well.

She looked disappointed. 'Oh well. Next time, perhaps.'

With a grin and a wink, she was out of the door.

TUESDAY

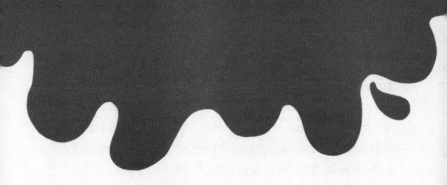

Morning

I Spoil Someone's Weight-loss Diet and am Accused of Murder

That night I dreamt that I was trapped inside a giant doughnut. I was trying to eat my way out but then Jane and Gamble started gobbling it . . . and when I screamed at them to stop my lungs filled with jam and I couldn't escape because my hands and feet were stuck and then –

I jolted awake, sweating, my bed covers tangled round my arms and legs. I touched my face – it was warm and sensitive but it no longer hurt. I was absolutely starving.

Speaking of which . . . It was half-past six in the

morning. No one else in the house would be up but it'd be rude not to satisfy my rumbling tummy with a teeny weeny pre-breakfast doughnut, wouldn't it?

I crept down to the kitchen and pulled a stool over to the top cupboard where Mum keeps the emergency doughnut. The box is always hidden behind the tea bags because Mum thinks I won't look there. I reached past them, expecting my fingers to bump against it at any moment but – *hang on* – it wasn't there.

'Looking for this, by any chance?' said Mum from the doorway.

I turned slowly around. Mum was wearing her nightie and dressing gown. She was holding a pink, shiny gift bag with tinsel and bows dangling off it.

'What's *that*?' I asked, climbing down off the stool.

'It's a doughnut,' said Mum.

'The *emergency* doughnut, you mean?' I said. 'Why's it wrapped up like a Christmas present? And how come you're up so early?'

Mum clapped her hands excitedly. 'I woke up suddenly an hour ago and the idea was right there in my brain: wouldn't it be cute if Roman gave a present to his girlfriend?'

'Oh,' I said. I was horrified. Jane would probably swallow it whole.

At that moment, Dad came bundling downstairs into the kitchen, his suit half on and toothpaste all round his mouth. 'Ah, you're awake! Brilliant news about the girlfriend!' he cried, slapping me on the shoulder. 'Now, quick tip. Never do what she says . . . or is it *always* do as she says . . .?'

Dad isn't good at advice.

Mum shook her head, 'Oh, fasten your trousers, Frank.' She handed me the gift bag. 'Right, Roman. Make sure you give it to Jane outside school so I can get a photo.'

'Definitely not,' I said.

'Nonsense,' said Dad. 'First girlfriend – this is a big moment. Gutted I'm going to miss it. Hey, Barbara, maybe you could get a video of her eating it as well.'

'Good idea,' said Mum.

I shuddered. 'You *really* don't want that,' I said. 'Maybe I should just save all this fuss and eat it myself?'

'It's no fuss,' said Mum. 'It's sweet that you've got a girlfriend.'

'I think she only came round yesterday for a doughnut,' I said.

'Nonsense,' said Mum. 'She wanted to see you.'

'Only because she felt bad for ignoring me after she got covered in wee,' I said.

'Wee?' said Mum.

Dad whistled. 'Wow. Things've changed since I was a lad.'

'You're meant to shower her with *gifts*, Roman,' said Mum, 'Not with . . .' Her voice tailed off.

'It wasn't my fault,' I said. 'Someone was throwing wee at me and I kind of *ducked*.'

'Very wise,' said Dad. 'A gentleman always puts himself first.'

Mum rolled her eyes. 'No, Frank. A gentleman puts his *lady* first. It's obvious: you owe Jane one, Roman. You *have* to give her this.'

And so, a couple of hours later, I wound up shuffling through the school gates with my hair greased down, wearing a tie and carrying the most embarrassing gift bag of all time. I turned around and Mum grinned at me from the other side of the fence, camera at the ready.

At least I'd persuaded her not to follow me onto the playground.

An Incredibly Hairy White Pencil Case

I didn't actually get the chance to give Jane her present straightaway. She was standing with her friends and they all huddled together and started giggling when I came through the gate. Mum gestured at me to go over to Jane. I stood behind a tree, pretending not to know who she was.

Thankfully, the bell soon rang and we all trooped inside. As I was hanging up my coat in the corridor, I tried to slip the gift bag with the doughnut into my rucksack. I was hoping Jane wouldn't have noticed it.

I should be so lucky.

'You look smart, Roman,' she said, practically yanking the gift bag out of my hands. 'A present? For me? Is this what I think it is? Oh, thank you!'

'I thought we could share it?' I offered. *Worth a try.*

Jane screwed up her face. 'Hmmm. I'm not sure. I think it's bad luck to share a present with the person who's just given it to you.'

'Oh,' I said. 'I've never heard th–'

'Trust me, it is,' she said quickly. 'You can sit with

me at playtime while I eat it, though. It'll be *so* romantic.'

Yes, I thought, *romantic . . . like watching feeding time at the zoo.*

At that moment, Rosie Taylor suddenly appeared. 'Everybody! Status update: Roman's bought Jane a present.'

Everyone else said, 'Oooooooooooh!' I felt myself blushing bright red.

'Present?' said Gamble, elbowing his way through. 'What present?'

Oh great.

Jane licked her lips. 'Well, if I know my Romy-womy, it'll be a big blob of raspberry jam, all wrapped up in yummy, scrummy Squidgy Splodge dough.'

'Where's mine?' said Gamble. His baked bean head was twitching angrily.

'Er, *you're* not his girlfriend,' said Jane.

'Shut your gob, toilet face,' replied Gamble, grabbing it off her. 'He promised me one yesterday.'

'*Do* something, Roman!' cried Jane. 'You're meant to be my boyfriend!'

Hmmm. I probably should do something, I thought. Then again, this was Darren Gamble we were talking about here. On his first day in school he told us all he'd once been arrested for headbutting a police car.

I decided not to intervene.

Jane huffed out her cheeks. She reached forward for the gift bag but Gamble ducked out of her way, pulled out the unwrapped doughnut, rubbed it under his armpits then offered it back to her. 'Still want it?'

Before she could answer, Mrs McDonald stomped into the cloakroom. 'What is the meaning of this?' she snarled.

Gamble innocently hung the gift bag on his peg. 'Nothing, miss.'

Rosie Taylor stepped forward. 'It was all Roman's fault.'

Typical.

'As if I wasn't having a bad enough morning already,' Mrs McDonald tutted. 'I'm not interested in your silly squabbles.'

'But . . .' said Jane.

Mrs McDonald raised a chubby little hand. 'I've enough problems of my own, thank you. All of you in class now.'

Jane looked like she was about to cry.

On his way past, Gamble shoved his face right

in front of mine. I don't want to be horrible but his breath smelled like – *erm* . . . imagine if an old lump of cheese learned how to fart and you might be halfway there.

I thought he was going to punch me or threaten me but instead he did something worse. Darren Gamble shook my hand. 'Thanks for the doughnut . . . *mate*,' he said.

Mate? Wonderful.

Thanks to the deadly doughnut, I was now 'mates' with the craziest kid in our school.

Inside our classroom, Mrs McDonald took the register in a flat, irritable voice. Jane was sobbing in her chair but Gamble wasn't bothered at all. He was bouncing up and down, waving his hand about. Next to him, Miss Clegg was filing her nails.

'What is it, Darren?' said Mrs McDonald, not looking up from the computer.

'Miss, you said you were having a bad morning. Why, miss? Were you drunk last night, miss?'

A few people tittered.

Mrs McDonald pursed her lips. 'If you must know, this is the reason why . . .'

She reached behind her desk and pulled out an enormous cage. It was so big it practically filled the front table. There was a big *wowwwww!* as everyone surged round it.

'Is it a rat?' said Gamble, pressing his face right against the bars. 'Do you want me to shoot it, miss? I can get my air rifle. Roman'll hold it still for me.'

'Certainly not,' said Mrs McDonald. She opened a little door on the cage and pulled out what looked like an incredibly hairy white pencil case. 'This is my prize-winning guinea pig, Mr Wiggles.'

'Oooh, yuck,' said Rosie Taylor. 'Rodents are disgusting.'

Mrs McDonald brushed its long, fluffy fur with a tiny silver comb. 'Actually, Mr Wiggles is a valuable pedigree piggy-wiggy. There is nothing disgusting about him. He's probably cleaner than some of the people in this class.'

I wasn't the only person who glanced at Gamble when she said this.

The hairy white pencil case tried to crawl up the sleeve of Mrs McDonald's cardigan. She pulled it out. 'Oooh, it tickles. He's always trying to play hide-and-seek.'

'Why's he in school, miss? Is summat wrong with him? Has he got worms like my dog?' said Gamble.

Mrs McDonald took a deep breath. The guinea pig tried to burrow under her sleeve again. 'Certainly not. I've had to bring him to school because – *well* . . . he gets lonely on his own and I've sacked his babysitter.'

A babysitter. For a guinea pig. *Good grief.*

'Why did you sack her, miss?' asked Gamble. 'Was she playing football with him as the ball?'

'No, of cour–'

'Did she nail him to the wall and throw darts at him?'

'Defin–'

'Did she tie him to a firework and shoot him into space?'

'Actually,' said Mrs McDonald, covering the guinea pig's ears, 'I gave the babysitter a special diet sheet for Mr Wiggles to stick to – smoked salmon, grapes, cherry tomatoes, organic orange juice. You know, the normal foods for a guinea pig . . .'

Normal? Mr Wiggles eats better than me!

'Anyway,' continued Mrs McDonald, 'she *must* have been feeding him unhealthy snacks instead. Look. This is what he used to look like . . .' She pointed at the framed picture of Mr Wiggles on her desk. 'And look at him now! He's obese.'

She held him up in the air to prove her point. A couple of people in the class gasped at the difference. In real life he looked *fairly* similar to the picture: i.e. like a Cornish pasty wrapped in a wizard's beard. However I have to say that, since the picture had been taken, he *did* look like he'd been given a few blasts with a bicycle pump.

I remembered her phone call at the aquarium. Mrs McDonald had been talking about someone putting on weight. I'd assumed she was talking about a person – a human – but she must've been talking about Mr Wiggles.

Mrs McDonald rubbed her nose against the guinea pig's nose. 'It's the British Guinea Pig Championships at the weekend. How can he defend his gold medal from last year when he's so overweight? The head teacher says I can keep him here to control his diet. It was that or I had the week off.'

Rosie Taylor put up her hand but didn't wait to be asked before speaking. 'Miss, you know that American singer, Indigo Termite?'

'No,' said Mrs McDonald, wearily.

'Well,' said Rosie, 'on secretcelebritygossip.com it said she lost eight stone in two weeks by eating only powdered egg shells and garlic. You should try that with your hamster.'

'Guinea pig,' huffed Mrs McDonald. 'And no, I will not. Those diets have terrible side effects. The BGPA – the British Guinea Pig Association – would never allow a guinea pig with bad breath to win the title.'

'Can I stroke him, miss?' Gamble asked.

'Under absolutely no circumstances,' said Mrs McDonald, placing the guinea pig carefully back into his cage and clipping the door shut. 'And that goes for everyone. Mr Wiggles has only just come back from his hair stylist.'

His hair stylist. *Yowsers.*

'Now,' said Mrs McDonald, carefully placing the cage next to the sink. 'In today's English lesson we *were* going to write about our aquarium trip but I've changed my mind. Instead we're going to write a letter of complaint to an irresponsible guinea pig-sitter . . .'

Good Man

We'd been working for about half the lesson. I'd written two paragraphs. Gamble (who'd insisted

70

on sitting next to me) had finished in three minutes. His letter read:

Dear Stoopid Cow
— you mess wiv Mrs McDonald's pet rat again an I'll smash yer face in.
Love Darren

He was now picking bogies out of his nose, rolling them into balls and placing them on his side of the table in a neat row. Miss Clegg was staring out of the window, pretending she wasn't listening to music through an earphone. Jane was already on her third page. She hadn't even looked at me since Gamble pinched her doughnut.

Meanwhile, Mrs McDonald showed no interest in any of us. She was standing over the guinea pig cage, pushing Mr Wiggles' fat rear end back onto his exercise wheel whenever he tried to get off it.

At this point, Mr Noblet came in. Mr Noblet is our headteacher. He's friendly and enthusiastic. Everyone likes him, even though he has a moustache and wears socks and sandals instead of shoes.

'Hey, guys. Sorry for invading your space,' said

Mr Noblet. 'Mind if I whizz an idea past all of you?'

'If you must,' sighed Mrs McDonald, closing the door of the cage and posting a piece of lettuce through the bars.

Mr Noblet gave her the thumbs up. 'So, every year after the tests are finished, we get Year Six to host a tea party for some senior citizens from the retirement home down the road,' he said. A few people shuffled in their chairs. He laughed. 'Don't worry. They won't bite.'

'One of them did last year,' yawned Miss Clegg.

'Well . . . yes . . .' said Mr Noblet. 'But they've promised not to bring *her* this time. Anyway – it's a wonderful chance to show off how great you all are. We'd love a few people to help Mrs McDonald to organise it.'

'Like I haven't got enough on my plate,' mumbled Mrs McDonald.

Mr Noblet clapped his hands. 'Come on, guys. Who's going to do something amazing today?'

Everyone suddenly became very interested in their shoes.

'Anybody . . .?'

Very slowly, Jane's hand went up. 'Will there be money to spend on snacks?'

Hmmm . . . I thought. I had a sneaky suspicion of what she was up to.

Mr Noblet tilted his head slightly. 'And why do you need to kn–'

'To give the old people a really lovely time,' she continued, quickly.

'A very kind thought,' said Mr Noblet. 'Of course the school will provide plates of biscuits for them.'

Jane thought for a moment then glanced very quickly at me. 'I think I'd like to do it,' she said. There was a funny look on her face, like a person who'd just remembered where they'd left an entire family bag of Monster Munch.

Rosie Taylor screwed up her face and shoved her hand up as well. I don't think she really wanted to do it but she doesn't like it when other people are in charge of things.

Then, next to me, Gamble's hand went up too.

'Just the two of you?' said Mrs McDonald, scanning the room.

'Three, miss,' said Gamble, bouncing around.

Mrs McDonald spoke over him. 'Only two girls. What about a boy?'

Gamble was straining so much he looked like his

neck might explode. 'I'm a boy, miss. Over here, Miss. I'll cook for 'em, miss!'

Mr Noblet looked over to Gamble. 'Yes. What about Da–'

'Trust me, Keith. Don't even go there,' Mrs McDonald said sharply.

'Yeah, we want to feed them, not poison them,' muttered Miss Clegg.

Gamble pushed back his chair and crawled under his table in a sulk.

'Is there. . . anyone else?' sighed Mr Noblet.

'Roman will do it,' said Jane.

'Er . . . what?' I said. Normally I try not to get involved in . . . well, *anything* really.

Mr Noblet squinted. 'Which one's Roman?'

Unbelievable. I know I'm pretty good at keeping my head down at school but come on – I've been coming here for seven years! I raised my hand.

Mr Noblet nodded as though suddenly remembering who I was. 'Ah. Great to have you aboard. If you're keen.'

I was about to say 'not really' when Jane piped up: 'He told me he'd love to.'

'Did I?' I said. *Why was she involving me in this?*

'Yes, remember?' she said, winking. Then she

dropped her voice to a whisper. 'There'll be snacks. And we can spend more time together.'

I tried to smile, my face burning as everyone in the class stared at me. 'That sounds . . . good.'

I really wasn't sure if this *was* actually good or not.

'Plus you owe me one,' she said.

This was *definitely* not good.

'I don't want Roman to help,' said Rosie. 'Him and Jane will spend the whole time eating doughnuts and planning their wedding.'

Mr Noblet acted as if he hadn't heard and gave me a double thumbs up. 'Good man for volunteering, Roland.'

'Roman,' I said, as Mr Noblet left the room.

Jane rubbed her hands together then went back to her work. The room was quiet again, apart from the sound of Mr Wiggles eating his lettuce and Gamble gnawing on a table leg.

Minus Fifty Doughnuts

At the start of lunchtime, and before I'd had the chance to escape, Jane chaired the first meeting of the Old People's Tea Party Committee (i.e. her, Rosie and me). It was an absolute disaster.

For a start, I was annoyed at being there. This wasn't because I don't like old people. It was because Tuesdays are the best days for school dinners. If you get in early, it's hot dogs followed by profiteroles (which are like doughnuts but filled with cream and covered in chocolate – not as good as the real thing but still, better than a kick in the throat). Obviously these are the popular choices so they run out fast. If you're late, all that's left is cheese omelette (looks and tastes like an old trainer insole), and fruit (pointless except in Starbursts and jam). The other two didn't seem bothered about this. I was doomed.

We sat down round a table. Mrs McDonald had put Mr Wiggles into one of those plastic balls that rodents run around in on the floor. She was lying down next to him, clapping her hands and saying, 'Let's hustle,' and 'Sweat is just the fat crying,' and 'Faster! You want to fit into that special Spider-Man costume Mummy made, don't you?'

(Yes, I thought the last one was a bit weird too.)

Mr Wiggles sat completely still, his flabby body spreading out across the bottom of the ball like a bag of custard.

'OK,' said Jane. 'Lots to organise, so let's get started. What's first?'

'Roman shouldn't be allowed to help,' Rosie said. She was brushing her hair and she paused for a moment to get rid of a tangle. 'He's weird and horrible.'

I said nothing. Although the last four words weren't very nice, I have to say I didn't mind the first bit.

'That's my boyfriend you're talking about,' said Jane. 'Anyway. Roman's agreed to provide the cakes for the tea party.'

'I have?' I said.

'Good. About time he did something nice,' Rosie said, taking a quick glance in her hand-held mirror to check her hair was perfect.

Jane ignored her. 'Yes, the school's offered to buy some biscuits but I think the old people deserve better than a few Rich Tea, don't you? You'll need to bring the money tomorrow.'

'Maybe we should vote on that,' I said.

'Well, you *did* let Darren Gamble steal my doughnut,' Jane said, smiling in a way that was kind *and* slightly threatening at the same time. 'So I vote that you should.'

'I agree with Jane,' said Rosie. 'Two votes to one. Cough up the dosh, sucker.'

'So . . . I've found out how many are coming,'

said Jane, 'and just the forty-seven doughnuts should do it.'

'Forty-seven?!' I spluttered. 'That's almost a million.'

Jane put on a baby voice. 'Romy-womy,' she said, 'you'll get the doughnuts, won't you? For me?'

There was a long pause.

'Ahem – and for the old people, of course,' she added quickly.

'But I don't *have* forty-seven doughnuts!' I protested.

'Forty-nine,' Jane replied.

'Hold on. You said for–'

Jane tickled me under my chin like I was a flipping donkey. 'Well, you might as well get two for me while you're at it.'

'Two?'

'You know – one to replace the one that Darren Gamble stole. And the other because, well . . . I just want another one.'

'But I don't have forty-*nine* doughnuts either!' I protested.

'You don't need the doughnuts, silly Romy-womy,' Jane said. 'You just need the *money* for the doughnuts.'

'How am I supposed to get hold of that sort of money?' I spluttered.

Rosie folded her arms. 'Told you he was nasty. Now he wants the old people to starve to death as well. That's it. Mrs McDonald!' she called, staring right at me. 'Mrs McDonald, Roman's trying to kill some old people.'

'Don't do that, Roman,' said Mrs McDonald, not looking up. Carefully, she rolled the exercise ball down a ramp she'd made out of dictionaries and atlases. It trundled across the floor, bashed into a chair leg then came to a stop. Mr Wiggles looked at her grumpily.

'OK, OK,' I said. 'I'll *try* but I can't prom–'

'Excellent,' said Jane. 'Don't forget the money tomorrow. Mrs McDonald said she'd go and buy them for us.'

Mrs McDonald rolled the ball back up to the top of the ramp and waved a hand to us. 'Yes, yes. Whatever. I've got to get loads of salad for Mr Wiggles anyway.'

'And you'd better give me your mobile number so I can contact you,' Jane said.

'Do you *really* need it?' I asked. My mobile phone is actually just my dad's old one. I've only ever had one text (from Mum) so I gave up charging it about three months ago. Ever since then it's been gathering dust at the back of my bedside drawer.

'Boyfriends and girlfriends should stay in touch at all times,' said Jane, passing me a piece of scrap paper.

I copied my number down for her. 'If I'm buying the doughnuts, what are you two going to do?'

'Well, I'm organising the whole thing,' said Jane.

Rosie flicked back her oh-so-wonderful hair. 'And I'm going to be the one who meets and greets the old people, of course, because I'm the most fabulous.'

I rolled my eyes.

'Well, there's no way we'd let a little freak like you near them, is there?' she said, making a 'Loser' sign with her hand.

'Everyone in the class will meet them,' said Mrs McDonald, shoving the exercise ball down the ramp again and still not looking over.

Rosie looked at me, her eyebrows raised. 'What? Even *that?*'

'Rosie, why are you being so mean to my boyfriend?' said Jane. 'Is it because you're jealous?'

Rosie's slug's-bum mouth tightened. 'What?'

'Well, Roman's mum said you used to want to marry him,' said Jane, innocently. 'I'm sorry if I've stolen him from you.'

'www.i'mgoingtopuke.com,' said Rosie. She turned up her nose and flounced out.

Jane put her hand over her mouth. 'Oops! Sensitive. Can't have her being mean to my Romy-womy, though, can I? Especially when you've got such an important job to do. Now what about the entertainment . . .'

I tuned out as Jane spouted on at me about sing-alongs and dance routines. How was I meant to get hold of enough money for forty-nine doughnuts by Friday? Plus *I* needed a doughnut for myself as well – I'd never gone a whole day without one before! I was worried that if I didn't get one soon there was a good chance I'd die.

I did some sums in my head. I had zero doughnuts and I needed fifty. Therefore, by my calculations, it turned out I officially owned *minus fifty* doughnuts. I tried to figure out what this looked like but it made my head hurt so I had to stop.

Eventually Mrs McDonald ended the meeting so she could go off to find some bubble wrap. She wanted to make Mr Wiggles a special sweatsuit to help him lose more weight when he did exercise. I don't think that guinea pigs actually sweat but I was so glad to escape that I didn't say anything.

Lunch was absolutely rubbish. There wasn't even any omelette left so all I got were cold chips and a couple of really depressed-looking fish fingers. Of course the profiteroles had all run out. In fact, after she'd stormed out of the meeting, Rosie had nabbed the last four. She spent ten minutes slowly eating them while looking right at me, just to rub it in. Then she announced to the whole room that she was full up and tipped the last one into the bin. I nearly cried.

I didn't realise that things were about to get worse.

Aren't Doughnuts Healthy?

When I came back into the classroom after lunch, there was a terrible row going on by Mr Wiggles' cage. Gamble was looking confused and holding a half-eaten doughnut in his hand. Mrs McDonald was looming over him, her face bright purple.

'What do you mean, you were giving him a treat?' she screamed. I noticed she had a tiny bubble-wrap waistcoat in her hand.

'I thought he might like something nice to eat,' shrugged Gamble. 'I thought you'd be pleased, miss.'

Inside the cage, I could see the fat guinea pig guzzling down the mangled-up chunks of doughnut that Gamble must've posted through the bars. Mrs McDonald opened the cage door and tried to take them off him.

'YOOOOOWWWWWW!' she screamed, suddenly yanking her hand out of the cage and shutting the door. She held her finger and shook her head. 'Mr Wiggles has never bitten me before. Never.'

Gamble shrugged again. 'He must like the dough-nut then.'

Mrs McDonald glared at him. 'I'm trying to get him to lose weight for the British Championships and you're stuffing him full of junk food.'

'"Junk food"?' asked Gamble, scratching an angry zit on his scalp. 'Aren't doughnuts healthy?'

'What?' cried Mrs McDonald.

'They're full of jam. Jam's fruit, innit,' he said.

Inside his cage, Mr Wiggles was chomping the doughnut down like crazy, his jaws whizzing up and down like a pneumatic drill.

'Doughnuts are deep-fried in oil and they're absolutely stuffed full of sugar,' said Mrs McDonald. 'Have you any idea what that much sugar could do to a delicate piggy-wiggy?'

This question was answered by Mr Wiggles. He hoovered up the last remaining crumbs of doughnut and stood still for a moment, his head jerking from side to side.

Then he went completely nuts.

It was terrifying.

Mr Wiggles charged round and round his cage in a whirlwind of sawdust, then flung himself against the bars. His eyes were wild and he was snapping at the metal with his teeth. There was red stuff all round his mouth (which was probably jam but looked like blood). The whole cage was rattling. We all took a step backwards.

Suddenly he flopped down and lay very still.

'Is it dead?' yawned Miss Clegg.

The guinea pig answered by snoring loudly.

'I get like that when I eat sugar, miss,' said Gamble. 'That's why I like it. I go crazy-wild then I have a big sleep. It's well good!'

Mrs McDonald snatched the remainder of the doughnut off Gamble, put it back in the gift bag and shoved it into the high cupboard above the sink where she keeps all the paints. 'Detention. Tomorrow,' she growled.

'Mrs McDonald,' said Rosie Taylor, 'it's not all

Darren's fault. *Roman* gave the doughnut to him.'

Mrs McDonald turned towards me. 'Detention for you too.'

I wanted to explain how unfair this was but suddenly Gamble grabbed me round the shoulder. 'Brilliant – best mates in detention together.'

I put my head in my hands. All I'd wanted yesterday was to eat a doughnut. Just one innocent jam doughnut. And now here I was: forced to organise an old people's party with my greedy pig of a girlfriend who would stop at nothing for more sweet treats, *and* in big trouble along with my new best mate, who just happened to be completely insane.

That deadly doughnut was slowly ruining my life.

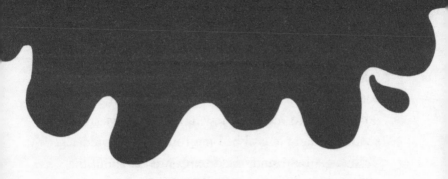

Evening

I Get Rich, Temporarily

'So, how was school?' asked Mum over dinner.

I shovelled a heap of mashed potato into my mouth and grunted. I didn't want her to know about the detention.

'Did your girlfriend like her present?' asked Dad.

Strangely enough, I was glad that he'd brought this up. I'd been wondering how I was going to ask them for the money.

'Yes,' I said. 'In fact, she'd love some more.'

'Oooh, how cute,' said Mum. 'I knew it'd work a treat.'

I cleared my throat. 'Er . . . fifty more, to be precise.'

Dad nearly spat out his dinner. '*Fifty!* What does she think we are, *made* of jam?'

'Sounds like she only wants you for your doughnuts,' Mum said, waving a forkful of steak pie at me.

'No, no, no,' I said, and I explained all about the old people's tea party. I decided not to explain that two of the fifty doughnuts were for Jane and one was for me.

'Oh, how lovely!' Mum cooed, giving me a huge sloppy kiss on the cheek. 'Such a kind young man – I'm so proud of you!'

Dad dipped into his wallet and handed me twenty quid right there and then. I couldn't believe it; I was loaded!

'All for a good cause, son,' he said. 'Now, speaking of which, I knew we'd run out so I picked something up at Gibson's on the way home . . .'

He went into the kitchen and came back with a small tray of Squidgy Splodge doughnuts just for us. This was terrific! I could've wept. I was going to eat my favourite snack *and* all of my doughnut-related problems were solved. Everything was brilliant!

That is, until the doorbell rang.

He's Clean

Gamble was standing on my doorstep. He was still in his school uniform and he was holding onto a dog by its lead. The dog was really scruffy. It was long and thin with patchy fur, and one of its eyes was milky. It was straining against its lead and making a really horrible wheezing sound.

'Wanna hang out . . . mate?' said Gamble, grinning.

Before I could make an excuse, the dog jumped up onto my chest and started licking my face. 'Yuck! Get it off me!' I said, wiping the slobber off my cheek. I hate to say this but its breath smelled slightly better than Gamble's.

Gamble pulled the dog down and sniffed the air. 'Are you eating dinner?' he asked. 'I'll have some.'

I tried to stop him but he pushed past me and headed towards the dining room.

When I got there, Mum and Dad were staring at Gamble and the dog, open-mouthed.

'Nice pad,' he said, looking round.

'This is Gamble . . . er, Darren . . . from school,' I said. 'He's new.'

'Er . . . hello, Darren,' said Mum. 'It's nice of you to drop in but we don't normally allow animals ins–'

Gamble scratched the dog behind its ears. 'Oh, don't worry about Scratchy here. He's clean.'

I looked at the dog and gulped. 'Are you *sure*?' I asked. 'It's . . . licking its bottom.'

'Oh, yeah,' replied Gamble, 'He does that a lot. It's the worms, you see . . .'

My mouth went dry and my stomach began to feel very shaky. I suddenly realised how Kevin 'The Vomcano' Harrison must feel on a long-distance coach journey. 'But you just let it . . . lick my face.'

'Can't stop him being friendly,' grinned Gamble.

'Urgh, gross,' I said, frantically rubbing my cheek with my sleeve.

'I'll fetch some wet wipes,' Mum said.

As soon as she stood up, Scratchy leapt onto her chair, put its paws onto the table, shoved its head into the Squidgy Splodge tray and dragged its tongue along all three of the doughnuts.

'Oh, come on!' I said. 'This is too much.'

'Wow! Doughnuts!' said Gamble, picking one up in his filthy hand. 'Are you eating 'em?'

The dog started scraping its bottom against the back of Mum's chair.

'I think I'll give it a miss,' I said.

'Not really hungry,' said Dad.

'Brilliant,' said Gamble, stuffing them into his pockets.

Scratchy farted triumphantly.

When Mum came back with the wet wipes and saw Scratchy on her chair she hit the roof. Gamble was asked to leave. He wasn't bothered at all. In fact, he seemed quite used to being thrown out of places.

Apart from a nasty smell (rotten eggs mixed with wet dog), all that he and Scratchy left behind was the Squidgy Splodge tray. Once again I was completely doughnutless. I was gutted about what Gamble had done. But, as Mum went round with the bleach spray and air freshener, I had an idea. I took the empty tray upstairs.

After washing my face six times I went to my room. My phone was charging on my desk – I'd dug it out and plugged it in when I came home from school. I sat down on my bed and switched it on. Straightaway it beeped three times. Three text messages in one go, Wow! That was three times more than I'd received in my whole life.

The text messages were:

Mum (from two months ago, which shows how often I use my phone):

Hello darling. Just wanted to send my lovely boy a big kiss. XXX

Delete.

Jane (today at 15:35):

Hi Roman. Quick reminder about the money for the doughnuts. Love your gf Jane x

Delete.

Jane (today at 15:37):

Why haven't you replied yet? I probably should mention that if you don't bring the money, our relationship will be over. X

Hmmm. I couldn't figure out whether or not this was a bad thing.

Delete.

I decided not to reply to either Jane or my mum. I only had three pounds and eight pence of credit left and I needed almost half of it for what I was planning.

When I'd seen the doughnut tray lying on the table, I'd remembered about the competition. Mum had mentioned it to Jane the day before.

On the side of the tray it said you had to send a text to Squidgy Splodge explaining why you should win in 160 characters or less. Texts cost £1.50 each. This might seem expensive but the winner would get a year's supply of doughnuts. For me, a year's supply would be loads – maybe a gazillion tonnes or something. This meant it was definitely good value for money.

I sat on my bed for about an hour, writing, deleting and changing my text until I was happy with it and it fit the 160 characters.

In the end I went with:

I jst want 2 eat dnut but bn stung by jfsh,told off 4 feeding fat rodent & forced 2 buy dnuts 4 OAPs.my GFs a pig & I may hav dogs bum worms in my mouth.Pls hlp

I wasn't sure if it made sense but it felt important to get everything in there. I needed the judges to feel sorry for me. Taking a deep breath, I pressed send.

I nervously fiddled with the phone. This was my big chance. The last two days had been awful but maybe whoever read the text would realise this and know that I deserved those doughnuts more than anyone else on the planet. Surely no one else would have a hard-luck story like mine? I had to win! I imagined the van . . . no, the lorry . . . no, the fleet of jumbo jets bringing me my year's supply of doughnuts. Me ripping open the first box, stuffing the delicious balls of joy into my mouth. Sitting there on a mountain of used trays, covered from head to toe in crumbs an–

BEEP!

YES! A text from Squidgy Splodge!

That was quick. They must've loved my message and decided immediately that I was the winner. I opened it excitedly.

Then my face dropped.

Sorry. You did not win. Please try again and keep enjoying the great taste of Squidgy Splodge.

And that was that.

I'd failed.

I flopped back onto the bed.

WEDNESDAY

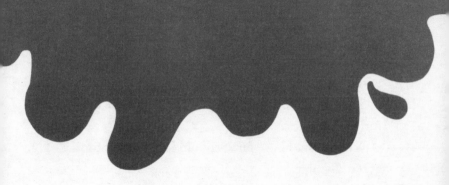

At School

I Give a Guinea Pig a Makeover (and My Teacher Has a Breakdown)

The next day I took my twenty pounds to Mrs McDonald. She was still cross from the day before so she put it in her desk drawer without looking at me. She spent the whole morning pushing Mr Wiggles round in his exercise ball and ignoring us while we did boring maths worksheets.

At lunchtime, Gamble and I had our detention. As soon as everyone else had gone outside, Mrs McDonald brought her shredding machine out of the big walk-in cupboard in the corner of the classroom. She plonked it down on my table, along with a massive stack of old paper.

'Shred that,' she said, flatly. 'I'll use it as bedding for Mr Wiggles.'

'What should I do, miss, should I shred stuff too?' asked Gamble.

'You know you're not allowed near sharp objects, Darren,' she replied. 'Not after what happened with those knitting needles.'

Gamble sniffed. 'That was an accident. And anyway, how was I supposed to know those Year One kids would get in my way?'

'Hmmm,' said Mrs McDonald. 'I'm off to prepare Mr Wiggles his salad. Miss Clegg will look after you while I'm gone.'

Miss Clegg rolled her eyes.

Jane was also in the classroom, along with Rosie. They were designing posters to advertise auditions for people to perform at the old people's tea party. Rosie was so delighted about me being in trouble that I thought she might actually explode.

As soon as Mrs McDonald had gone, Miss Clegg stood up. 'I'm off to the toilet,' she yawned. 'No talking.'

And away she went. We were alone. I fed the

first sheet of paper into the top of the shredding machine. There was a loud whirring noise as the sharp metal teeth of the shredder pulled the paper down, chewed it up and spat the bits into the box underneath. It was brilliant fun! I did another, and another, and another. It didn't feel like a punishment at all. In fact, it was the most fun I'd had since before the doughnut disaster at the aquarium.

'Can I have a go?' said Gamble.

'No,' I said. 'We're already in enough trouble.'

Plus I'm enjoying it too much.

Gamble stood there for a moment, looking about and twitching. Then without warning he scrambled up onto the sink, his feet inches from the guinea pig cage.

'What are you doing?' I asked. 'You'll knock Mr Wiggles onto the floor.'

Gamble was standing right in front of the cupboard so he had to bend down in order to open the door past his head. 'I'm getting my doughnut back,' he said. 'Me and Scratchy enjoyed the ones you gave us yesterday.'

From my seat, I could see that the gift bag with the half-doughnut inside was right at the back of the cupboard, behind the powder paints. A very uneasy feeling started building in my stomach as Gamble reached into the cupboard. The cage was right beneath the cupboard door so Gamble had to stand to the side of it and stretch across on his tiptoes, feeling for the doughnut with his fingertips.

'I'll tell,' said Rosie.

'Oh shut it, you sweaty butt-waffle,' said Gamble over his shoulder.

Rosie's mouth opened and closed a few times like a fish.

Butt-waffle? I wasn't *quite* sure what this meant, but nonetheless I think it described Rosie pretty well.

'Yeah, butt out, *butt-waffle*,' said Jane. Then she smiled at Gamble, who was now teetering danger-ously over the cage. 'Please can I have a bit too, Darren?'

Unbelievable! Jane had turned bad. And desperate – after all, that *was* the doughnut Gamble had put in his armpit. She was starting to give me the creeps a little bit.

'Got it!' cried Gamble joyfully.

'*Yesss!*' hissed Jane.

Then everything went wrong.

You know when people talk about things

happening in slow motion? Well, that's exactly what happened right then. The next three seconds seemed to last a lifetime.

Gamble pulled the gift bag towards him . . .

↓

and his sleeve caught a small pot of blue powder paint . . .

↓

which slipped off the shelf . . .

↓

and somersaulted through the air for what felt like hours. . .

↓

before landing upside-down on top of the cage and releasing a massive blue cloud . . .

↓

which slowly settled on top of Mr Wiggles.

This was not good.

With the gift bag swinging in his hand, Gamble hopped down to the floor and peered in at Mr Wiggles. 'Whoops,' he said.

I rushed over to the guinea pig cage. 'Whoops?' I said incredulously. '*Whoops?* Is that all you can say? Darren, the guinea pig is blue!'

'I'm going to find Mrs McDonald. You're all getting done. This is great,' said Rosie, skipping out of the room with a flick of her hair.

'Oh no!' cried Jane. 'Please, Roman, tell Mrs McDonald it was nothing to do with me! My parents are so strict, they'll kill me and . . .'

Jane began to cry.

Gamble suddenly became calm and business-like. I guess he'd been in a lot of sticky situations before. 'Right. *You*: stop blubbing,' he said to Jane. 'Go and find Mrs McDonald and stall her.'

Jane nodded meekly, and did as she was told.

Gamble pulled out the doughnut and threw the gift bag to one side. 'And *you*: help me sort your mess out.'

I peered into the cage. '*My* mess?'

Gamble shrugged. 'Your doughnut.'

'Bu–'

'No buts,' said Gamble. 'Lucky I'm here to help.'

Before I could argue with him, he ripped off a chunk of doughnut then opened the cage, lifted Mr Wiggles up and set him on the palm of his hand. The guinea pig gobbled up its snack hungrily.

'Don't give him *more*!' I said. 'We're already in trouble for feeding him. That's why we're in detention!'

'My uncle always says: "Sometimes you've got to break a few little laws to get away with breaking the big ones",' said Gamble, grinning.

I didn't really want to know any more about Gamble's uncle but I guess I could see his point. At least the doughnut was keeping Mr Wiggles still while we thought of something to do about his blue fur.

Gamble nodded towards the little silver comb that was next to the cage. I picked it up and carefully brushed as much of the paint as possible out of Mr Wiggles' coat. It helped, but there was a big patch on his back where the powder was tangled right down to his skin.

Gamble placed Mr Wiggles onto the draining board and examined him. 'Think she'll notice?'

I looked at him in amazement. 'Darren,' I said, 'he's got a bright blue Mohican.'

'Cool. Guinea pig punk!' he grinned. 'We can pierce its nose too. I'll get the staple gun.'

'Don't you dare,' I warned him. I wasn't sure if he was joking or not.

Mr Wiggles was wriggling about impatiently so Gamble broke him off another piece of doughnut. 'Hey!' he said, 'did you see that Squidgy Splodge are running a competition? I noticed on that tray you had in your house *and* I saw a poster when I nicked off school last week.'

I sighed. Gamble's like this all the time. He has the attention span of a caterpillar. 'I know, but there's no point. It's a big swizz. And anyway, this isn't the time. We've got about one minute to figure out how we're going to clean the paint off this rodent.'

'Easy,' said Gamble. 'We can lick it off him. I eat paint all the time.'

Before I could stop him, Gamble's face was hovering above Mr Wiggles' back, his tongue hanging out.

I managed to stop him just in time. What a complete maniac! I mean, the paint was bad enough but what would Mrs McDonald do if she found us *licking* her pet guinea pig?

'There's got to be something else we can try,' I said. 'There's a dishwasher in the staffroom,' said

Gamble. He sounded completely serious.

'This can't be happening,' I said.

'We could give it a haircut,' said Gamble.

'And how will we explain *that* to Mrs McDonald?'

'Say it got a shock and its hair all fell out,' he said. 'Do you have any better ideas?'

Well, I thought, *perhaps if we only trim off the blue bits . . .*

'You'll have to do it, though,' said Gamble. 'I'm not allowed to use scissors.'

Not being allowed to do something had never seemed to hold Gamble back before, but it was probably for the best if I took charge. I took a pair of scissors from the block by the sink. As carefully as I could, I held a lock of fur on Mr Wiggles' back and snipped. A blue-white wisp fell away.

Good start, I thought. *Maybe this could work . . .*

I took a deep breath and trimmed a bit more. And a bit more. And a bit more. Then I stood back and admired my handiwork. Well, I *had* managed to get rid of all the blue paint. But then again . . .

'He looks like a monk,' said Gamble.

He was right. There was a large, hairless circle in the middle of Mr Wiggles' back. 'This is really bad,' I said.

'We could give it a combover,' said Gamble. 'You just brush the hair over the bald patch. My dad does it.'

'Your dad's a *human*,' I said. Although, looking at Gamble, I realised that might not necessarily be the case . . .

'Fine,' said Gamble. 'Looks like it's down to me to save the day. *Again*. Give the scissors here.'

Then, with absolutely no precision or control, he started *snip-snip-snipping* away at poor Mr Wiggles, who calmly stood there, munching more and more doughnut from Gamble's other hand. I couldn't see anything until finally Gamble stood back to admire his work. '*Cor!*' he exclaimed. 'She was right about him being fat!'

I put my hand in front of my mouth. It was now clear why Gamble was banned from using scissors. 'It's official,' I said, 'we're dead.'

'Rubbish. We got rid of all the paint.'

This was true – there wasn't even a single speck of blue paint left on the guinea pig.

Unfortunately there was no *white hair* left on him either. Mr Wiggles was completely and utterly bald. He looked like a miniature hippo!

'All that's left are his whiskers,' I said sadly.

'Oh, yeah. You're right,' said Gamble. And with two quick snips, he took them off as well.

'Stop it!' I said, snatching the scissors out of his hand. 'You've ruined Mr Wiggles.'

Gamble screwed up his face. 'You know . . . you might be right. I reckon Mrs McDonald probably preferred him hairy.'

I wrung my hands together. 'This is *really* bad. We'll own up and take our punishment and then . . .'

'Don't be thick,' said Gamble, punching me in the shoulder, 'no way I'm lettin' my best mate get in trouble. Let's get some glue.'

'Glue?'

Gamble plonked Mr Wiggles down on the side and grabbed a pot of PVA out of the cupboard. 'Yep. We'll spread glue all over his back then roll him in the white hair. She'll never know the difference!'

'He's a guinea pig,' I said, 'not a coconut macaroon.'

At that moment Rosie Taylor appeared at the door. 'Just thought I'd let you know, Mrs McDonald's on her way,' she said, a big smarmy grin across her face. 'And trending on Twitter at the moment? "You two getting done"!'

With an evil snigger, she swept back outside.

And so the worst plan in the history of the world quickly took shape.

Two Guilty Monkeys

I swear Rosie Taylor had never looked so pleased as when she returned with Mrs McDonald a minute later. Jane Dixon was behind them, her face pale.

Gamble and I stood to attention next to each other, blocking off Mr Wiggles' cage. 'Hi, miss,' said Gamble, hiding the glue pot behind his back.

We both smiled as innocently as we could.

Mrs McDonald frowned. 'Why are you grinning like that? You look like two guilty monkeys.'

'More like a pair of serial killers,' yawned Miss Clegg, lolloping into the room.

'Weren't you supposed to be watch–' began Mrs McDonald but Miss Clegg interrupted her.

'Needed the loo. Curry last night,' she said, wafting her hand up and down.

'*Urgh*. T-M-G,' said Rosie. 'Too Much *Grim-*formation.'

'Miss,' said Jane, 'please can we go somewhere else and talk about the old people's tea party?'

'What's that by the sink?' said Mrs McDonald.

I felt the sweat on my neck turn cold.

'Doughnut, miss,' said Gamble, casually. 'Guess what? There's a competition, right, and I'm gonna win a year's supply and share it with you, miss, because I love you, miss.'

'Very kind of you, Darren but what's the doughnut doing there?' Mrs McDonald said. Her eyes narrowed. 'Did you take it out of the cupboard? I thought I'd told you . . .'

She stalked towards us like a hungry leopard.

Gamble and I huddled closer together. It felt like a cold fist was twisting my intestines.

'Don't worry, miss,' said Gamble, calmly, 'we saved you a bit, look.'

He thrust the well-nibbled doughnut under Mrs McDonald's nose and she snatched it off him. 'I'm not interested in – *EEEEEEEEEEEEEEE-EEEEEEEEEEEEK*!'

She'd seen Mr Wiggles.

Mrs McDonald flung the lump of doughnut onto the worktop and shoved past me and Gamble. Then she pulled open the cage door and scooped the guinea pig up. 'WHAT HAVE YOU DONE?!' she yelled. Her face had actually turned purple and her eyes were bulging out like ping-pong balls.

'Dunno what you're talking about, miss,' said Gamble innocently.

Mrs McDonald was panting heavily. Her free hand gripped the sink for support. 'He's . . . he's . . .'

'Shall I get you the behaviour book, miss?' said Rosie Taylor.

Mrs McDonald let out a howl from somewhere deep in her chest.

Gamble looked surprised. 'Are you . . . *angry*, miss?'

I could see where she was coming from. Mr Wiggles was bald, which was bad enough, but on his skin were random patches of stuck-on hair and crusty bits of glue. Unfortunately, he'd also stuck to some pencil shavings, some glitter and a few crumbs of doughnut along the way, as well as a couple of pink feathers that Gamble thought might look nice. He looked like he'd just had a fight with the art cupboard.

'What have you done?' screamed Mrs McDonald again.

I looked at my shoes. 'I'm sorry.'

Mrs McDonald placed Mr Wiggles down next to the sink. '"Sorry"? SORRY? He's ruined! I'll be the laughing stock of the British Championships!'

'You could get him a wig, miss,' said Gamble helpfully.

Mrs McDonald didn't seem to hear him. She was pacing up and down, talking loudly to herself. 'He'll have to retire now. Two years of training and grooming wasted. WASTED!'

'What will you do with him now you can't put him in shows, miss?' said Gamble, revving up with excitement again. 'Will you eat him? We had this cat once, right, and . . .'

'BE QUIET, YOU AWFUL CHILD!' screeched Mrs McDonald, jabbing Gamble in the chest with a stubby finger.

'Oh, please, miss,' said Gamble, his lip wobbling. 'Don't be like that, miss. I was just trying to help. I couldn't stand it if you were mad at me, miss.'

Gamble looked like he was about to cry. I couldn't believe it but I actually felt *sorry* for him. 'Mrs McDonald, it was me as well,' I said, looking at the floor.

'You too? You little –' she screamed.

Now, I'll never know the reasons for what happened next. Maybe Mr Wiggles understood what Gamble had said about his cat. Maybe he was scared of the noise of Mrs McDonald screaming like that. Or maybe he just saw the doughnut, noticed no one was looking at him and thought he'd make a break for it.

Anyway, with surprising speed for such a fat rodent, he darted forward and bit off a wodge of the doughnut. Then he shot away behind the sink and along the worktop.

Mrs McDonald dived towards him but she was too late. Mr Wiggles had already squeezed himself through the hole in the wall where the pipes go. She hauled open the door of the cupboard under the sink and desperately pulled out the paintbrushes and pallets and glue sticks but there was no sign of him. From the other side of the hollow wall we could hear a scuffling noise, which became quieter and quieter before turning to silence.

'He's . . . gone,' said Mrs McDonald, softly.

Miss Clegg sniffed. 'They always go somewhere peaceful to die.'

Not really helpful, I thought.

There was a thud as Mrs McDonald fainted and collapsed to the floor.

Flat Out

Rosie ran off and returned with Mr Noblet. 'What's going down, guys?' he asked.

'Well . . .' began Rosie.

Gamble stamped on her foot to shut her up and told *his* version of what happened. By the time he'd finished his story – about how the guinea pig had gone for Mrs McDonald's throat and he'd had to beat it off with the doughnut – Mrs McDonald had woken up.

'Where am I?' she said, in a floaty voice. 'Where's Mr Wiggles? Who shaved him?'

'Crumbs,' said Mr Noblet, biting his lip. 'She's delirious. Did you see anything, Miss Clegg?'

From over Miss Clegg's shoulder, I could see that she'd used her phone to take a photo of Mrs McDonald when she was lying on the ground. She was just posting it on Facebook with the tag: 'My teacher, working flat out'.

'Nope,' she said, sliding her phone into her pocket. 'I was in the bog.'

Mr Noblet looked like he'd just swallowed something sour.

'Covered in glitter and feathers . . .' said Mrs McDonald, her head lolling about.

'You poor thing,' said Mr Noblet, helping Mrs McDonald to her feet. 'You've been working too hard. Home to rest, I think. I'll take your class. Miss Clegg – a hand.'

Miss Clegg tutted loudly and huffed over to the stricken Mrs McDonald. Together, they helped her out of the classroom.

When they'd gone, Rosie Taylor turned on Gamble and angrily pushed her hair back. 'You're lying and I'm going to tell Mr Noblet what really happened.'

'Try it and I'll smash yer teeth out,' said Gamble.

'Yeah, Rosie,' said Jane. 'Button it. Or else.'

I mentally added 'threatening people' to the list of things Jane had started doing since I'd given her a piece of the deadly doughnut on Monday.

'Maybe we should try to get Mr Wiggles back?' I said. 'You know, for Mrs McDonald.'

'Good idea,' said Gamble. 'You still owe me a doughnut, though. This one's covered in guinea pig spit. Even *I* won't eat that.'

And with that, he threw the remaining lump into the bin. Even though the doughnut had been in Gamble's armpit and Mr Wiggles' mouth, I felt my stomach muscles clench. Binning doughnuts is a horrible crime. It's like taking a beautiful painting and blowing your nose with it.

'And don't forget you owe me forty-nine,' Jane said, fluttering her eyelashes.

Added to the one I was desperate for myself, I

was now on *minus fifty-one* doughnuts. I bit my lip. There was another problem: my twenty pounds was in Mrs McDonald's desk. If she'd gone home, how could she go to the shop to get them for me?

Things were getting worse by the second.

For the rest of the day, Mr Noblet got us to design a machine we'd like to invent. This is the kind of doss-about lesson that headteachers always give you so they can sit at the front and get on with paperwork.

By the way, I don't want to sound big-headed but my machine was brilliant. It was called The Multiblaster. All you had to do was zap something with a laser and it'd make hundreds of copies of it. I thought it'd be useful for getting all the extra doughnuts I needed. Rosie Taylor's invention was a set of X-ray glasses that could see through walls and round corners. Kevin Harrison invented a special sick bag that turned your puke into money. Gamble designed a new missile for blowing up cows (don't ask), while Jane came up with a handheld device that could tell you where your boyfriend was at all times. I wasn't sure I liked her invention.

The room was totally quiet apart from Gamble talking at Miss Clegg. 'What are you doing tonight, miss? Have you got a date with your boyfriend?'

'None of your business.'

'Have you got a boyfriend, miss? I bet you have. You're not as beautiful as Mrs McDonald but there must be someone out there who fancies you, miss.'

'If you must know, Darren, I'm going to the supermarket. Now can we please colour in these cow's brains and get this over with.'

Gamble stood up. At first Miss Clegg looked like she was going to stop him but then she just huffed out her cheeks and gave up. He walked over to me. 'Hey, Roman. Wanna hang out after school?'

'Ummm . . .' I said, concentrating on my machine and hoping he'd get bored and bother someone else.

'I've got this awesome idea to get the doughnuts.'

'Yuck!' said Rosie. 'Something stinks round here.'

'Shut it, fart-burger,' said Gamble.

'You're gross,' Rosie hissed. 'I'm going to sharpen my pencil. Don't you dare touch my stuff with your greasy fingers while I'm gone.'

Spying on everyone else's work on the way, Rosie walked the long way round to the bin. As soon as she'd stopped, Gamble flung one of her rubbers at her. It smacked her on the back of her head, which caused her to drop her pencil sharpener into the bin.

'Bullseye!' he said, rushing back to his place. 'High five, Miss Clegg!'

Miss Clegg looked at his hand like he'd just used it to clean out a toilet. 'No throwing, Darren,' she said unconvincingly.

'Hey – everything groovy out there, guys?' said Mr Noblet, glancing up from his work.

Gamble glared at Rosie. She pursed her lips, picked some imaginary bits of rubber out of her hair and reached into the bin.

What happened next was incredible.

There was a clang as the bin flew onto its side. About one millisecond later, Rosie let out a deafening scream and shot into the air, waving her hand about. It took me a moment to realise there was something hanging off the end of her finger.

It was something very fat, very pink and very bald, with all kinds of stuff stuck to it.

Mr Wiggles!

He must have sniffed out the doughnut then crawled into the bin to get it.

'GET IT OFF ME!' Rosie shrieked, swinging the fat bald guinea pig round and round her head. Mr Wiggles hung on, his teeth sunk deeply into her flesh.

'Put him back in the cage!' I cried. This was my chance to finally do something good.

'Chop her finger off!' called out Gamble.

'Don't they carry rabies?' asked Miss Clegg.

'I feel sick,' said Kevin *The Vomcano* Harrison, turning a funny shade of green.

Rosie was going completely nuts by now, flapping her hand back and forth so the guinea pig was a total blur. 'I hate rats! I hate rats!' she squealed.

'Stay still,' said Mr Noblet, grabbing Mr Wiggles and trying to pull him off Rosie's hand. The guinea pig must've let go because all of a sudden Mr Noblet was stumbling backwards, holding Mr Wiggles up in the air like he was the World Cup. But then he slipped on the lumpy puddle that Kevin 'The Vomcano' Harrison had just created on the floor. Mr Noblet's feet flew up in the air above his head and he tumbled over in a heap.

Mr Wiggles flopped onto the floor and zigzagged back across the classroom as fast as his fat little body could manage. When he reached Rosie, she actually went to stamp on him but Gamble rugby-tackled her out of the way just in time.

Meanwhile, Mr Wiggles grabbed the rest of the doughnut from the floor by the bin and squeezed through a gap in the skirting board, dragging the doughnut behind him.

For a moment, the only sound in the room was Rosie sobbing.

'Awesome,' said Gamble.

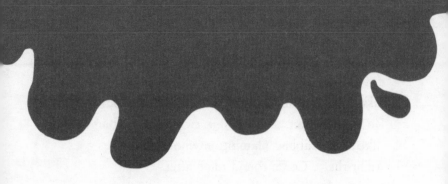

After School

I Am Forced to Try Out a New Way of Shopping

At three-twenty, Gamble was waiting for me by the gates on the way out of school, a big goofy grin across his face.

'You need doughnuts, right?'

'Yes. Fifty-one of them.'

'Fifty-two,' he said. 'Mr Wiggles loves 'em so I'm gonna use one as bait and get him back.'

For Gamble this was actually good thinking.

'At home we use chocolate to catch mice and rats then I electrocute 'em and run 'em over on my skateboard and that sort of stuff, but I won't do that with Mr Wiggles cos I love Mrs McDonald.'

'Where are we going to get the doughnuts?' I asked, trying to ignore most of what he'd just said.

'Supermarket,' said Gamble, twitching and blinking like a sick rabbit. 'S'next to my house. The bus goes right there. Come round mine after.'

'I don't think I'd be allowed,' I said.

Well, not without a set of injections first.

'Give us yer mobile,' he said.

Reluctantly I took it out of my rucksack and handed it over. He searched the numbers and dialled my house. Someone answered and Gamble started speaking. 'All right, Mrs Roman's mum, it's Darren Gamble. Roman's coming round my house for tea and we're having roast pheasant.'

I heard Mum's muffled voice say, 'Ooooh, very posh.'

'Yeah,' said Gamble. 'Dad ran it over in his car last night.'

I slapped a hand against my forehead. *Wow.* I knew Gamble was a bit on the scuzzy side but I'd no idea he *ate roadkill.*

I could hear Mum over the line asking to speak to me.

Gamble seemed to weigh this up for a few seconds.

'Nah,' he said, then he hung up on her. I was about to say that this was pretty rude when his face lit up. 'Look – here comes the bus.'

A normal person stops a bus by putting out their hand. Gamble's method was a little bit . . . *well* . . . different. Just as the bus was coming past at full pelt, he leapt out into the middle of the road in front of it, screaming and waving his arms around.

I could see the panic in the driver's eyes. He slammed on his brakes, screeching to a halt inches in front of Gamble. About a second later, a tiny dog crashed against the inside of the windscreen and slithered down it, legs spread wide against the glass.

'Cool,' said Gamble. He skipped round and hopped up through the open doors.

'What is wrong with your brain?' snarled the driver. He seemed pretty angry.

Gamble ignored the question. I think he'd probably been asked it before. 'You shouldn't have braked so hard,' he said. 'Look at that poor dog.'

The tiny dog was drunkenly staggering round in circles on the floor. An extremely old woman scooped it up and gave Gamble a dirty look. Gamble grinned at her. 'Probably best to keep a hold of his lead,' he said.

The old woman said something extraordinarily rude. I'd never heard a woman in her eighties swear before then. I guess that's the effect Gamble has on people.

'Hurry up and pay your fare or I'll kick you off,' said the driver.

'I'm really sorry but we don't have any money,' I said.

Gamble pulled a twenty-pound note out of his pocket.

'Where did you get that?' I said.

'Saw Mrs McDonald put it in her desk so I nicked it at playtime, innit,' he said, as though this was a normal thing to do.

I tried to figure out if this was wrong or not – I mean, I knew it was wrong but it *was* my twenty-pound note and we *were* going to use it to get the doughnuts, as planned. Maybe it wasn't *totally* wrong . . .

'I don't give change,' said the driver.

'Doesn't matter,' said Gamble, poking the twenty quid into the slot. On buses round here, you put your money straight into a machine and it drops down into a safe.

'Yes it does!' I cried. 'We need that!'

It was too late. The driver had already pressed the button. There was a *ch-ching* sound. The money dropped out of the glass slot and disappeared.

'Oh yeah,' said Gamble. 'I forgot.'

The tickets were printed and the doors closed.

The other people on there (mainly old) looked just as cross as the lady with the dog. A couple of them were picking themselves up off the floor. A handbag had spilled all the way down the aisle, sending boiled sweets and loose change rolling everywhere. Gamble didn't seem to notice.

'And how are we supposed to get the doughnuts now?' I asked him as we sat down.

'No problem,' said Gamble. 'There's always begging. Or the five-fingered discount.'

'The *what*?' I said. I didn't like the sound of this.

Gamble wiggled his fingers in the air. 'You know, shoplifting. I do it all the time.'

He said this cheerfully, like it was nothing out of the ordinary. *I've got loads of hobbies,* I could imagine him saying: *skateboarding, cricket, shoplifting, murdering dolphins – you know, all the usual stuff.*

I turned my back on him, hunched my shoulders and put my head against the cold window. If I hadn't tried to eat the deadly doughnut on Monday, I wouldn't be mates with Gamble, I wouldn't have a girlfriend who was hassling me, I wouldn't own minus fifty-two doughnuts, and I wouldn't be about to launch myself into a life of crime.

Surely the deadly doughnut couldn't cause me any more problems.

Could it?

I think we all know the answer to that one . . .

The Chance of a Lifetime

When we reached the supermarket, the good news was that we didn't need to beg or steal. The bad news was that things turned out much, much worse.

As soon as we got off the bus, Gamble spotted Miss Clegg pushing her trolley into the shop. 'Miss Clegg!' he screamed. 'Can we sit in your trolley, miss? Can you push us round, miss? Miss! MISS!'

I've never seen the face that people pull when they find out the hard way that a cat has gone to the toilet in their shoe. However, I'm guessing it's pretty similar to the face Miss Clegg pulled when she saw Gamble bounding towards her. With surprising speed, she zipped off into the shop, slaloming in and out of other shoppers until she was out of sight.

'Mustn't have heard me,' said Gamble as he wandered back.

I said nothing.

Just as Gamble reached me, a young man with slicked-back hair and a shiny suit stepped between us. He had a dark orange fake tan and a huge grin that showed off his dazzlingly white teeth. 'Congratulations!' he said, putting a hand on Gamble's shoulder. In his other hand he was holding a camcorder.

A young woman appeared next to him. She was also smartly dressed and was pushing a trolley with balloons attached to it. 'You're our one thousandth customer today!' she beamed.

'Really?' I said. I tried to work out how likely this was. In the last thirty seconds, around forty people had gone into the store. If it had been open since six a.m. then that would mean at least . . .

Gamble interrupted my thoughts. 'What do we win?' he said.

The young man's smile was still fixed on his face. 'Well,' he said, 'your incredible prize is . . . a trolley dash for you and your friend here!'

'Oh, brilliant!' said Gamble, bouncing about excitedly. 'Er . . . what's one of them?'

'You have five minutes,' said the woman, pulling a stopwatch out of her pocket. 'Run inside, fill this trolley with as much stuff as you can and get back here before the time runs out. If you make it back in time, you keep everything in the trolley. For free!'

'Wow!' said Gamble.

'Are you sure this is for real?' I said, frowning. On close inspection, the man and woman only looked about seventeen, and they weren't wearing badges or anything.

For the first time, the man's smile cracked a bit. 'Hey. Would we be allowed to stand here if it wasn't?'

'Hmmm, I guess not,' I said. It was a pretty good point.

'Don't throw away the chance of a lifetime,' said the woman.

This was another good point.

'Your time starts . . . now!'

She pushed a button on the stopwatch and, before I could stop him, Gamble was sprinting off into the shop with the trolley.

'If I was you, I'd go too,' said the man, pointing the camcorder at Gamble's back. 'Otherwise he'll only fill it with things that *he* wants.'

This was the best point of all.

Now, part of me did think that this was too good to be true. But we were desperate and I wanted to believe that my luck had changed. And I could imagine Gamble stuffing the trolley with rat poison, worm medicine for dogs, and flammable household cleaning products.

What did I have to lose? I took a deep breath and ran after him.

For two minutes I searched up and down the store but Gamble was nowhere to be found. Time was ticking away so I decided to change my tactics. I'd go straight to the doughnuts, grab as many as I could carry and *then* find him.

Luckily, it was the supermarket where Mum does the family shop so I knew my way round. Within a minute I was standing on my favourite aisle.

The Cake Aisle

The cake aisle at the supermarket is amazing. It's kind of like how I imagine heaven to be. There are millions of different cakes – Swiss rolls, chocolate party cakes, jam tarts. Best of all, though, there's the biggest Squidgy Splodge doughnut cabinet you have ever seen. It's about five metres long and it's beautiful

– it has a huge lit-up sign above it and three warm shelves absolutely bursting with every Squidgy Splodge flavour there is. My tongue was hanging out as I let my eyes drift across the glistening rows of glorious treats:

- **Plain Glazed Ring** – an excellent beginner's doughnut but not for the expert.

- **Choco-Vanilla Dream Ring with Nut Sprinkles** – perfect for a birthday party but not suitable for everyday use.

- **Banoffee Bad Boy** – chocolate, toffee, crushed biscuit, banana and cream – a truly excellent all-rounder. And it contains fruit so it's perfect for athletes and anyone watching their weight.

- **Lemon Curd** – a revolting lump of pure disappointment.

- **Raspberry Jam** – the greatest doughnut of them all. The Ferrari of deep-fried doughy treats.

And then I saw them, sitting there on the shelf in a great big mountain of loveliness:

I pressed my face against the glass and examined them longingly. It'd been so long since I'd last tasted one. I felt like I'd been lost in the desert and had finally found water. All I wanted to do was shove my head inside the cabinet and stuff myself until my stomach exploded.

This wouldn't help me in the long run, though, so I had to control myself. There was no time to count them; I just needed to get as many as I could. I gathered up a load of trays and boxes, filled them with doughnuts and stacked them on the floor. Then, when there were more than I could carry, I shoved loose doughnuts into my rucksack, up my jumper and into every single pocket.

A lady frowned at me as she ambled along the aisle but I ignored her – there wasn't time to explain. I picked up the pile of boxes, trying not to squash the doughnuts under my clothes, and staggered off to find Gamble. There must've been about six boxes in my arms and I could barely see over the top of them. The sugar and oil were hot against my skin but I didn't care any more. I was desperate and it'd be worth it.

I didn't notice that the frowning lady was following me.

Code Red Emergency

I'd been up and down about six aisles with no sign

of Gamble when an announcement came over the loudspeakers: 'All security staff to Checkout Four. Code red emergency!'

This could only mean one thing: *Gamble*.

My heart pounding, I rushed there as quickly as I could.

At Checkout Four, everything was going nuts. The assistant was screaming. There were security guards piling in from every direction. The trolley with the balloon on it was off to the side, absolutely stacked full of iPads, mobile phones and games consoles. I'm not joking, there must've been about ten thousand pounds' worth of stuff in there.

But that wasn't the worst thing.

'Good grief,' I said.

Gamble was standing *on top* of the conveyer belt, crushing a bunch of bananas and a couple of vanilla slices beneath his shoes. Teeth gritted and eyes wild, he was attempting to wrench the till off the desk.

The *till*, for heaven's sake. I mean, they'd said we could put anything into our trolley but surely *that* wasn't included? I had to admire his guts but it *was* a bit much. It was like going to an all-you-can-eat Chinese buffet and trying to eat the waiter's leg.

The security guards couldn't get at him because the checkout was blocked with trolleys. In the background, the man and woman from outside were grinning and filming him on their camcorder.

Unfortunately for Gamble the till seemed to be bolted in place so he started slapping the buttons until eventually the drawer flew open. Just as he began shoving fistfuls of banknotes into his pockets, a huge security guard fought his way through and dragged him off the conveyer belt. Gamble was flipped onto the guard's shoulder and carried off, kicking and yelling.

'Leave me alone!' Gamble screamed, ten-pound notes fluttering everywhere as the guard stomped off down the shop. 'I'm on a trolley dash! You're wasting my time!'

A few customers scrabbled on the floor for the dropped banknotes while the other security guards tried to stop them.

I looked over at the man and the woman with the camcorder. They were filming me now. The woman pointed at her watch. 'Thirty seconds left,' she mouthed.

I felt *really* bad for Gamble. What would they do to him? There'd obviously been a misunderstanding.

The last thing I heard him shout as he disappeared through a door was, 'Get to the front of the shop, Roman! Quickly!'

I really wanted to help him but what could I do? If I didn't get back before the time ran out we wouldn't win anything . . . Gamble would be furious if he didn't get his prize. And what about the doughnuts? This was our only hope. I could always try to help Gamble afterwards.

Gathering up the doughnuts and tipping them into Gamble's abandoned trolley, I set off. I hadn't taken three steps before I felt a firm hand on my shoulder.

'Store detective,' said a strict-sounding woman's voice. 'Security! We've got ourselves another one.'

I spun round. It was the lady who'd frowned at me on the cake aisle. Suddenly I found myself face-to-face – well, OK, face-to-stomach – with three enormous security guards.

'Caught him red-handed, emptying out the Squidgy Splodge cabinet earlier,' said the store detective. 'Empty your pockets.'

'But . . .' I started.

'Now!' she snapped.

Reluctantly, I did as I was told.

As I dropped the last doughnut into the trolley, the shop manager pushed his way to the front. He was a short, round man with a red face and a bald head. 'Unbelievable. Shove him in the holding room with the other one and call the police.'

'I won a trolley dash!' I protested.

'Oh, that old one,' snapped the manager. 'I've heard it all before.'

'Honestly – I'm with my friend who was the thousandth customer,' I explained. 'We won a trolley dash. You can ask those people over there.'

When I looked over, though, the man and woman had disappeared.

'Save it for the coppers,' said the manager.

Two enormous hands were hooked under my armpits and I was led away from the trolley. But we hadn't gone far when a sleepy-sounding voice said, 'Er . . . where do you think you're taking him?'

The guards stopped. We all turned round.

Miss Clegg was standing there with her trolley. I couldn't help but notice that it was filled with toilet rolls and small boxes of something called 'WIND-BREAK – *tablets for the control of flatulence*'.

'What's it to do with you?' said one of the security guards.

'Well,' yawned Miss Clegg, 'he hasn't stolen anything, has he? I mean, unless he gets to the door, you don't *know* that he's not going to pay for it all.'

The guards loosened their grip on me.

'Ahem . . .' said one, scratching his head.

'Well, erm . . .' said the other.

Miss Clegg took a step towards me and placed her hand on my arm. 'For all you know, he might've been getting this stuff for me. So you should let him go.'

One of the guards began massaging his neck. The other started moving imaginary dust around the floor with his foot.

Finally the manager stepped forward and snapped: 'Right! Get out of here and don't come back. You're barred.'

'How will I get my doughnuts?' I cried. This was awful – like being banned from living.

'You've got five seconds to leave of your own accord or I call the police,' growled the manager.

I definitely didn't want to be arrested. Maybe I could come back in disguise or something?

I quickly thanked Miss Clegg for helping me.

'I was going to do the same for Darren,' she said, 'but then again . . .'

The security guards escorted me to the exit so I had no chance to find out where Gamble was. Before I knew it, I was outside. I ran all the way home.

Completely Out of Hand

When I got back half an hour later, I decided not to tell my parents that I'd been to the supermarket or what had happened to Dad's twenty pounds. This meant I couldn't say anything about Gamble, even though I was worried sick. As far as Mum knew, I'd been round at his house the whole time. Of course, she wanted to know everything about it so I had to make it all up. The conversation went like this:

'What was his house like?'

'Really nice.'

'Was it? Oh. Maybe I'll go with you next time to meet his parents.'

I gulped. This was a disaster. If she did, then she'd definitely find out I'd been lying to her. I hadn't even met Gamble's parents myself, and I only had a vague idea of where he lived. I started to panic.

'Well . . . actually it wasn't all that nice.'

'Oh?'

Think. Think.

'There was a . . . horse in the living room.'

Where did that come from?

'A *horse?*'

I'm going to have to stick with it now.

'Er . . . yes. A big horse.'

'Good grief. Was it all right? Do you want me to call the RSPCA?'

Argh – too much. Don't let her do that. Everyone'll know it was a massive lie.

'No, no. It was really happy. It was . . . watching *Countdown* and . . . smoking and . . . eating cheesy Wotsits.'

Mum's mouth made a perfect O shape.

Did I just say Gamble keeps a smoking horse in his living room?

'And did you eat the pheasant his dad squashed with his car?'

'Yes.'

'Really?'

'Well . . . I had a bit. You know. To be polite.'

'Oh, good. Was it . . . OK?'

'Fine. A little bit . . . um . . . Tarmac-y.'

'Maybe next time you go I'll give you a packed lunch.'

'Good idea.'

'And some wet wipes.'

Before I could say anything even more stupid, I escaped to my room. I went to check my phone then realised that Gamble hadn't given it back to me.

Gamble.

Where would he be? I imagined him locked in a dark, damp cell, with nothing to eat but a crust of stale bread.

I felt terrible. He might be a total loony but he's *my* loony.

And he wasn't the only one who was trapped either. I now had no money to buy the fifty-two doughnuts I needed: Jane was going to go bananas at me. Rosie Taylor would probably find a way of blaming me for Mr Wiggles attacking her. And Mrs McDonald would *definitely* blame me for her prize piggy-wiggy having escaped in the first place.

What a disaster. If only I hadn't tried to eat that doughnut on Monday, none of this would've happened.

THURSDAY

Morning

Girlfriend Trouble and a Rocket Launch Disaster

I was so worried about Gamble that once again I hardly slept. In the morning I dragged my feet to school, the whole time imagining what would happen when Mrs McDonald took the register:

No Darren today. Does anybody know *where he is?*

Yes, miss. He's in prison.

Ah well. It was always going to happen sometime, I suppose . . .

As I trudged through the school gates, someone slapped me on the back of my head. 'Gotcha!'

I spun round. *Gamble!*

'I'm so pleased you're all right,' I cried. I was going to hug him but then thought it might be a bit much. Plus I was wearing a clean coat. 'You're free! What happ–'

Gamble spoke over me. 'Well, the security guy took me to this office, right, and I was ready to use my ninja skills but then another security guard brought those two people in from outside who gave us the trolley, right, and it turned out they were playing a trick on us and filming it to put on YouTube so they had to let me go, innit.'

'The scumbags!' I said. 'I knew there was something funny about it.'

'But that's not all, see,' said Gamble, twitching like a mad badger. 'So I said "I'm telling the police you trapped me in a room cos that's kidnap."'

'What did they say?'

'They said, "OK, you can take something from the trolley." So I said, "I'll have an iPad then, innit."'

'Wow. Did they let you have it?'

'No,' he said, bitterly. 'But they let me have a doughnut.'

His face brightened up and he pulled the doughnut out of his coat pocket. Oh, it looked beautiful – like a glorious ball of jammy delight. I reached out to touch it but he slapped my hand away. 'Not a chance. I'm saving it for a special lady.'

Just then, Jane appeared at my shoulder. 'Hi, handsome,' she said.

'Morning, Jane,' I replied.

Jane pursed her lips. 'Actually, I was talking to Darren.'

I gulped. '*Gamble?* Handsome? But . . .'

'Tut tut, Roman. Don't be nasty about my new boyfriend,' said Jane.

'Your new *what*?' I said.

Don't get me wrong, it wasn't like I really *enjoyed* having Jane as my girlfriend, but . . .

'I'm informing you that I've dumped you and now I'm going out with Darren,' she said. 'You heard him – I'm his *special lady.*'

'Wow,' said Gamble, looking surprised, 'What can I say? The ladies love my swagger.'

'But . . . but . . . you *can't* go out with *that,*' I said to her.

'Ignore my *ex*,' said Jane, dragging Gamble away by the arm. 'He's just jealous. Now when can we share your doughnut?'

She was shameless!

Rosie came right up to me. 'Relationship status update,' she announced: 'Roman has been DUMPED!'

She pranced away cackling. The bell rang. As I trudged round to the classroom, I had a good think about everything. I was pretty sad about being ditched but surely Jane couldn't expect me to get those two doughnuts for her now. And surely she couldn't expect me to buy the forty-seven doughnuts for the old people's tea party either. She'd have to get them herself – or get her new *boyfriend* to get them. And, since Gamble had a doughnut of his own and a girlfriend, he wouldn't be wanting two off me either.

Maybe this wasn't all that bad. In fact, it was brilliant! I was in the clear.

By the time I got to class I was practically hopping up and down.

Crazy Lady

On Thursday mornings Mrs McDonald has her planning time so Mr Noblet takes us for science and PE. Normally Mrs McDonald works at home when she's planning, but on this Thursday she was at the door to the classroom having a massive row with one of the school cleaners.

'I'm meant to have finished by the time the children get here,' moaned the cleaner. 'I've *got* to vacuum the carpet.'

'Over my dead body,' said Mrs McDonald. 'My Mr Wiggles is on the loose somewhere in there. If I let you in, you'll suck him up the tube.'

'But . . .'

Mrs McDonald raised her finger. 'In fact, he's always crawling into small spaces. He's probably inside your vacuum cleaner already. I demand you take it to pieces this instant.'

Mr Noblet arrived. 'Mrs McDonald, please. We'll find Mr Wiggles.'

The cleaner was already walking away, muttering something about a crazy lady.

Gamble bounced straight up to Mrs McDonald. 'Guess what, miss? Cos you're my favourite teacher, I've brought you this, miss.'

He held out his doughnut to her.

Jane put her hand on his shoulder. 'Darren. Darling. I thought that was for *us*.'

Gamble didn't even look at Jane. 'Didn't say that.'

'But you said you'd saved the doughnut for a special lady,' she whined. 'I thought I was –'

'Can it, turtle breath. There's only one special

lady in my life and that's my Mrs McDonald, innit. And anyway – I know you fancy me and everything but I ain't gonna nick my best mate's chick, am I?'

Jane stormed off into the classroom and flopped down in her chair. I noticed her breathe into her hand and hold it up to her nose to check if her breath really *did* smell of turtles. *HA!*

'Darren,' said Mrs McDonald, sternly, 'it's your fault Mr Wiggles escaped in the first place. I'll never forgive you so don't try to get back in my good books by giving me cakes.'

'No, miss, it's not for you, miss,' said Gamble. 'See, I've been thinking that Mr Wiggles loves doughnuts, right, so I'm gonna put this in his cage. We'll leave the door open then close it behind him when he comes back, miss.'

Mrs McDonald's face suddenly seemed to soften. 'Oh, Darren. How sweet. I'd kiss you . . . if it weren't for . . . you know . . .'

The fleas? The worms? The smell?

'I understand, miss. We'll get him back. Promise,' said Gamble, blinking proudly.

Mrs McDonald wiped a tear from her eye.

When we were inside the classroom, Mr Noblet

got us to look for Mr Wiggles before our science lesson started. 'Don't forget, guys, he likes hiding in small spaces so use your incredible eyes.'

The whole class, and Mrs McDonald and Mr Noblet, searched everywhere, which was way better than doing science. The only person who didn't help was Miss Clegg, who sat in a chair, flicking through a magazine. We looked in the cupboards, behind the furniture, under the books on the shelves, even in the drawers. There was no sign of him.

After ten minutes, Mr Noblet told us to stop. 'Looks like he's pretty well hidden,' he said. 'But I did find *something* in the cupboard we could use for our science lesson.'

He pulled out a large box with a picture of an air rocket on it – you know, one of those ones where you stamp on a foot pump and it fires the rocket up into the sky.

'Cool!' said everyone.

'Let's take it out and give it a bash,' said Mr Noblet. 'Give Mrs McDonald some space to continue the search.'

Everyone cheered.

'Can I come?' said Gamble.

'No,' yawned Miss Clegg, putting her magazine back into her handbag. 'You know you don't *do* science any more, Darren.'

'*Awwww*, s'not fair. I wanna be an astronaut.'

Gamble was banned from science after a mini-beast lesson on his second day at the school when he put a centipede into Kevin Harrison's lunchbox (which caused the biggest Vom-cano eruption of all time). Since then, every week Miss Clegg takes him for a walk round the school grounds while we have science.

Grumbling and kicking the furniture, Gamble followed her out of the room.

Flying Pigs

Since we did the exams, school's become a piece of cake – aquarium trips, letters to guinea pig-sitters, inventing machines and doing simple maths worksheets. And this science lesson was the easiest yet. It was meant to be about gravity but all we had to do was troop out onto the field and watch Mr Noblet play with an air rocket.

Mr Noblet pulled a foot pump out of the box and joined it to a tube. The tube led to the rocket's launch pad, which had a thick pipe sticking up from it that the rocket slotted on to.

As Mr Noblet prepared to launch it, Gamble walked past with Miss Clegg. 'Can I jump on it, miss, can I?'

'No, Darren,' answered Miss Clegg, yawning. 'You'll only break it.'

'Huh. S'not fair,' he grumbled.

When Gamble was a decent distance away, we counted down from ten then Mr Noblet jumped on the foot pump and we watched the rocket shoot up into the sky.

Everyone was cheering. Their eyes followed the rocket as it climbed higher and higher. It was pretty ace, so I don't know *why* I glanced back over at the launch pad, but I did. And what I saw there made my tummy do a backflip.

A tiny little bald head was poking out of the top of the launch-pipe.

Mr Wiggles!

Of course! He must've crawled into it back in the cupboard. Why didn't anyone check before we used it? Mrs McDonald had been going on about him hiding in small spaces the whole time. Still, at least he was OK.

'Mr Noblet!' I cried but he couldn't hear me because everyone was howling as the rocket swooped down towards a tree.

I pushed through the rest of the class towards the launch pad. Mr Wiggles was scrabbling to escape from the tube but his fat body must've been stuck fast. I was almost close enough to touch him when . . .

'DARREN! Come back here!' cried Miss Clegg from somewhere.

Good grief! Gamble was charging towards the launch pad too. He mustn't have noticed Mr Wiggles and he wasn't looking where he was going. 'Stop me jumping on it now, Cleggy!' he shouted over his shoulder.

'But the rocket's not even on it!' groaned Miss Clegg.

'Don't care!' shouted Gamble back at her.

I tried to call out but it was too late.

'Ha ha! Divebomb!' yelled Gamble, leaping through the air.

I glanced from Gamble to Mr Wiggles. I swear the guinea pig looked straight into my eyes, just as Gamble's feet slammed onto the foot pump.

FUTTTT-OOOOOFFFFFF!

If you've ever wondered what a guinea pig sounds like when it's fired sixty feet into the air from a narrow tube, *that's* it.

'Good grief,' I said, as Mr Wiggles shot up and up, his fat pink body spinning through hundreds of somersaults until he was a tiny speck in the sky.

A couple of other people seemed to notice, nudging each other and pointing upwards.

'Oh no!' gasped Mr Noblet, squinting up into the sky. 'Mr Wiggles!'

One of the girls squealed.

Then something awful happened.

This was a lesson about *gravity*, after all.

Mr Wiggles began to plummet.

He was heading straight for the playground. He'd be splattered like a dropped pie.

'Do something!' shouted Gamble, who had stumbled backwards and was now lying on the ground.

I sprinted as fast as I could, my eyes locked on his little body as it fell, faster and faster ahead of me. Twenty feet up . . . fifteen . . . ten . . . five . . .

Desperately I dived forward, eyes closed, hands stretched out as far as they'd go.

SLAP!

At the exact moment I face-planted into the tarmac, I felt the guinea pig plop into my hands.

I'd caught Mr Wiggles!

'YESSSSS!' I screamed, opening my eyes. I could hardly even feel the pain in my face. Mr Wiggles was safe. This was amazing! In seven years of PE, I've never even caught a cold, and here I was saving a guinea pig's life. Mrs McDonald would be over the moon.

I pulled him towards my face. '*Woo-hooo!*' I said to him. 'You beauty!'

Without warning, Mr Wiggles lurched forward and bit me right on the nose. Seriously, talk about thanks! As I howled in pain, the evil little creature wriggled out of my hand and scampered across the playground. By the time I'd chased after him he was round the corner and out of sight.

How's My Boyfriend?

After Rosie ran inside to fetch her, Mrs McDonald marched outside and started shaking me by the shoulders and screaming at me to tell her what had happened to Mr Wiggles and where he'd gone. She seemed to think it was my fault that he was still missing. Honestly! In the end Mr Noblet had to prise her hands off me and tell her to go inside and rest.

But that wasn't the end of it. When we went back to the classroom, the doughnut that Gamble had left as bait was gone but the cage was empty. This meant Mr Wiggles must've come back into the classroom, stolen it and taken it off somewhere while Mrs McDonald was outside.

Apparently this was my fault too because she'd only stopped watching the cage to come outside and tell me off. So she went completely ape at me again.

In fact, Mrs McDonald was so angry that Mr Noblet sent us out for an early playtime to give her time to cool off. I went outside and sat on a bench on my own, rubbing my sore nose and cheeks. Yet another injury to my face caused by the deadly doughnut. Soon I'd be so hideous I'd have to start wearing a mask.

Jane came and sat next to me.

'Hi, Romy,' she grinned. 'How's my *boyfriend*?'

I turned my back on her. Even though I was pretty happy that she wasn't my girlfriend any more (it meant I no longer 'owned' minus fifty-two doughnuts), I guessed that I was meant to act upset.

'I don't know,' I said over my shoulder, 'why don't you go and find him?'

Jane laughed. 'Romy-womy,' she said, 'I didn't dump you for Darren – he's revolting.'

I tightened my lips.

'Come on. Remember when he went to the toilet behind the football goals?'

Disgustingly enough, this was actually true. Gamble got in mega-trouble for it but he said he only did it to 'mark his territory' so that wolves and bears wouldn't come into the school grounds and 'maul the children'.

She turned my shoulders around so I was facing her. 'I only went out with him so I could share his doughnut with you,' she said.

I wasn't sure how to feel about this.

'So, obviously,' she said, twizzling her hair around her little finger, 'you'll be helping at the auditions this lunchtime.'

'The what?'

'The auditions for people who want to perform at the tea party.'

'I hadn't really . . .'

'. . . *and* you'll still be bringing in the doughnuts for the old people tomorrow . . .'

'I think that will be totally imp–'

'. . . not to mention the two you promised me as well.'

This was awful. I was almost back where I started.

'I don't think I can do that,' I said firmly.

Jane didn't seem to listen. 'And maybe one more to celebrate us getting back together.'

I tried to speak but this time nothing came out.

'I knew I could count on you,' she said, giving me a peck on the cheek. 'See you at lunchtime.'

Out With the Dead Wood

PE was a disaster. We were practising fielding skills with Mr Noblet and guess what? I didn't catch a single tennis ball for the entire hour. Typical!

Afterwards, I ate my lunch slowly. This was partly so I could be late for the auditions and partly because it was chocolate sponge for dessert. Chocolate sponge is exactly the same as the normal sponge they serve but it's brown. It takes ages to eat as it's always as dry as a lizard's underpants.

When I got to the practice room, a group of barefooted Year Five girls were huddled in the corner. Kevin 'The Vomcano' Harrison was sitting on the carpet, looking dejected and pressing the keys on his trumpet. Jane was standing alone in the middle of the room.

'You're late, Roman. Where have you been?' snapped Jane, barely looking at me. I was about to open my mouth when she continued: 'Unless the answer is "getting the doughnuts for the tea party" then don't bother to say anything.'

Wow. She was in a really bad mood all of a sudden.

I decided to say something. 'I was eating.'

Jane tutted loudly and turned to face me. Her eyebrows were locked together like a pair of fighting snakes. 'Huh. Typical. Why is everyone trying to ruin my life?'

I took a step backwards. I'd never seen her so stressed.

One of the muscles in Jane's cheek was flickering. She clapped her hands and shouted over to the Year Five girls. 'Now come on, you lot. Are we *finally* going to do this dance without looking like a bunch of baby giraffes being electrocuted?'

The Year Five girls rolled their eyes at each other and slowly stood in a line in the middle of the room.

I didn't really like the way Jane was acting. But still, I was her boyfriend, even though I didn't really seem to have any say in this matter. *Maybe I should do something boyfriendly,* I thought. *I know . . .*

'Are you . . . *OK?*' I said.

It turned out this was a bad idea.

Jane spun round to face me so quickly I had to jump backwards. 'No, I'm not OK! We've got one day left till the tea party and in the last five minutes, *everything's* gone wrong with the entertainment. First the Year Two recorder group dropped out because they didn't like being told to raise their game . . .'

'You told them they sounded like a bunch of chimpanzees whistling through their noses,' said one of the Year Five girls flatly. 'They're only little.'

Jane blinked, trying to ignore her. 'Then *Kevin* here tells me that, *actually,* he's only been playing the trumpet for a fortnight.'

Kevin fingered the keys. 'I only know two notes. And I've not really got the hang of them yet. Plus I get sick when I'm nervous.'

'On top of that,' said Jane, her hands on her hips, 'the Year Five dance troupe has all the elegance of a bunch of overweight builders stamping on cockroaches in their work boots! How are we supposed to entertain these old folk?'

The Year Five girls looked at each other

open-mouthed. 'That's it,' said one of them, stepping forward. 'We're not being spoken to like that. Come on, girls.'

They all grabbed up their shoes and marched out of the room

'Fine!' cried Jane after them. 'Run away. Out with the dead wood. Pathetic!'

As soon as the door had closed, though, her shoulders crumpled and she began to cry. 'Oh, Roman,' she sobbed, flinging her arms around me, 'I just wanted everything to be perfect, so the old people could have a good time. And *everything's* gone wrong. All I'm left with is Kevin playing a fire engine siren.'

'I'm not even sure I can do that without throwing up,' said Kevin sadly.

Jane pulled her head away from my shoulder and wiped her nose with a tissue. 'Tell me you won't let me down, Roman. Tell me I can count on you to get those doughnuts.'

I felt really awkward and uncomfortable. I wasn't expecting to be hugged. My arms were crossed in front of my chest and I was doing my best to pull away. At the same time – and even though she had been seriously horrible – she *was* my girlfriend. And she needed me. Surely I could do *something* to make her feel better.

'Yes,' I said, hoping that she'd let go of me.

Unfortunately, this made Jane squeeze me even tighter. 'Oh, thank you, Roman! At least the old folk will have something to eat, even if the entertainment *is* rubbish.'

I gulped. What had I done?

Kevin cleared his throat. 'Should I practise the fire engine siren again?'

Right then the door opened and Darren Gamble walked in, followed by Miss Clegg. 'I'm here for the auditions, innit,' he announced.

Jane began to cry again. 'Just when I thought things couldn't get any worse.'

Gamble sniffed. 'Don't be sad just cos I dumped you – I love 'em and leave 'em. That's what I do.'

'Get rid of him, Roman,' Jane ordered through her tears.

'Maybe we should just see what he can do?' I said. I was starting to feel bad about how everyone treats Gamble like he's got bubonic plague. Mostly he's just a bit excitable but at least he *tries* to do the right thing. And I'm certain – OK, reasonably certain – that he's *not* got the bubonic plague.

Jane wiped her eyes and took a very deep breath. 'Fine. What's your . . . *ahem* . . . talent?' she said.

'I'm a proper well good singer, me,' said Gamble, grinning. 'My uncle says I sing like a mole.'

'Can moles si–' I started to ask.

'What *exactly* are you going to sing?' asked Jane, interrupting me. 'Aren't you into heavy metal music?'

'Yep,' said Gamble. 'I was gonna sing this proper mad tune by Cannibal Death Crew called "Brain Sandwich" but then I thought the old people probably wouldn't be into that.'

Jane slapped her hand across her eyes. 'Tell me this isn't happening.'

Gamble grinned. 'So instead I'm gonna sing "Baa, Baa, Black Sheep".'

'Baa . . . Baa . . . Black Sheep?' asked Jane. She suddenly started laughing like a crazy person. 'Go on then. Let's hear it. Why not?'

'This is going to be *amazing*,' said Miss Clegg, sarcastically.

Now, I'd never heard Gamble sing before but I expected him to sound very similar to a live rabbit being ironed. I closed my eyes as he took a deep breath and launched into his song.

And then something incredible happened.

He was absolutely *brilliant*.

Seriously, his voice was soft and gentle like a breeze through a dandelion clock, and there was this kind of deep sadness to it that just gripped you.

Go on, Gamble! I thought, *You show them!*

Miss Clegg, Jane and I stood there, our mouths gaping open, as he finished the first verse.

'I was *not* expecting *that*,' said Jane.

Even Miss Clegg was moved to comment. 'Hmmm. Not bad.'

'See? Told you,' Gamble said, shrugging. Then he kind of ruined everything by snorting loudly then spitting out a huge blob of something that looked like cottage cheese onto the carpet.

'Wow,' I said.

'Amazing,' said Jane. 'Just . . . don't do the last bit for the old people.'

'I can't promise anything,' said Gamble, rubbing it in with his foot. 'But I'll try.'

'Thank you,' said Jane. 'Well, that's the entertainment sorted. The old people will love him.' She kissed me on the cheek. 'Now we only need the doughnuts.'

After School

I Get a Lift in a Getaway Van

After school I walked slowly home, trying to figure out how I was going to get the fifty-one – no, *fifty-two* – doughnuts I needed by the next day. There's no way Mum and Dad would give me any more money and I'd raided my piggy bank so many times in the past that there were more IOUs in there than coins.

Maybe I could sell my hair to a wigmaker, I thought, *or perhaps someone would buy me as a slave.*

Nope. I had to face facts: I'd failed.

Gamble came up behind me and rubbed his knuckles on the back of my head.

'Still need those doughnuts?' he said, walking alongside me. 'I can get 'em for you. There's a little Squidgy Splodge cabinet at Gibson's.'

Gibson's is a local shop halfway between my house and school. It's where Dad bought the doughnut that Gamble's dog ate the other night.

'Yeah I know,' I said. In fact, there are Squidgy Splodge cabinets in loads of shops and petrol stations – I know where practically every single one in the whole town is. 'The problem is, I don't have any money.'

Gamble sniffed. 'You don't need any. My brother Spud used to do a paper round for Gibson and I helped him out every day. Gibson still owes us a week's wages. You can borrow the money if you want.'

'Wow . . .' I said. 'But . . . *why?*'

Gamble shrugged. 'You're my mate and you let me sing today and anyway *I* want one more doughnut to help Mrs McDonald get her guinea pig back. Come on.' He sped up suddenly.

I couldn't believe it. Even though I was now on minus fifty-two doughnuts, this was a *really nice* thing for him to do. 'Hey! Wait for me!' I yelled, and ran with Gamble all the way to Gibson's.

A Blue Transit Van

The door to the shop was locked. We peered through the glass together. The Squidgy Splodge cabinet was glowing like a magical treasure chest but there was no one around.

'Do you think he's closed for the day?' I said.

'Nah,' said Gamble. 'He never takes a day off – not even when he had measles. He's probably on the loo. We can go round the back. Me and Spud used to do it all the time.'

I wasn't too sure about this but I was so desperate for the doughnuts that I shrugged and followed him down the driveway. Outside the back of the shop, a blue transit van was parked with its side doors open.

'Oh, I see. The delivery van's here,' said Gamble. 'He always locks up for a minute while he goes through the order. He doesn't like to get ripped off, see.'

I walked alongside the van and looked inside – it was absolutely crammed full of boxes of sweets, chocolates, crisps and . . . right there, at the top, TWO MASSIVE BOXES OF SQUIDGY SPLODGE DOUGHNUTS! The word 'GIBSON'S' was scrawled across the boxes in marker pen.

This was brilliant. All my problems were solved. There'd easily be enough doughnuts to tempt back Mr Wiggles, get Jane off my case, feed the old folk *and* have enough left over for me and Gamble. All we had to do was agree the deal with Mr Gibson.

Gamble opened the back door of the shop. 'Mr Gibson! It's me – Spud Gamble's brother!'

There was no answer.

Gamble shouted again.

Still nothing.

'How well do you know him, Darren?' I asked.

Gamble scratched a big red spot on his scalp. 'Er . . . Last time I saw him was probably when he sacked Spud from his paper round.'

I frowned. He hadn't mentioned anything about *that*. 'Why did he sack him?'

'Oh, it was nothing,' said Gamble. 'This dog tried to bite Spud when he was delivering the paper.'

'And he sacked him for that?' I asked. 'Bit unfair.'

'Nah,' said Gamble. 'He sacked him for weeing on the dog through the letterbox.'

'You're kidding!' I said, even though I knew that he wasn't. 'And you've not spoken to him since?' No wonder he wasn't opening the door.

'Yep,' said Gamble. Then he raised a finger. 'Oh,

actually, no. He told Spud he'd have to wait a week for his wages, so we came down the next day and set off a load of fireworks in the shop.'

I took a really deep breath. 'I'm sorry. I thought you just said you set off some fireworks *inside* his shop.'

'Yeah. You can't let people push you around.'

A terrible feeling grew in my stomach. What if Mr Gibson had seen us coming? What if he'd been so terrified of Gamble vandalising his shop again that he'd locked the doors? What if he was inside now with the delivery driver, hiding behind the counter?

If that were the case, we'd never own those doughnuts.

Mr Gibson would only open up again when he was certain we were miles away. And if I came back later he'd be bound to recognise me – what if he banned me from his shop for knowing Gamble?

I bit my lip.

There *were* two boxes in the van, after all.

'Exactly how much money does he owe your brother?' I asked.

'Twenty-eight quid.'

I quickly did some maths in my head. Mr Gibson sells doughnuts at one pound fifty for four. There are thirty-two in a box so one box would be . . . twelve pounds, I think, so two whole boxes would cost . . . er . . . twenty-four pounds. If we took both boxes and called it quits on the money he owed Spud, Mr Gibson would end up with four pounds more than they were worth.

I reckon.

It's not stealing, I told myself. We'd be doing it for old age pensioners. Plus I could come in tomorrow without Gamble and explain. And if Mr Gibson didn't like it, I could pay him back every week out of my own pocket money.

I know it might seem a bit naughty, but I was desperate and I was certain it would solve all our problems.

It turned out I was very, very wrong.

Go! Go! Go!

Gamble hopped up into the back of the van and made a flight of stairs out of crates of fizzy drinks. He climbed up it and grabbed the Squidgy Splodge boxes off the top.

'We should write Mr Gibson a note,' I said.

'Good idea,' said Gamble, pointing to the corner

of the van. 'Is that a bit of paper poking out from under that old blanket?'

I pulled myself up into the van, lifted up the blanket and . . . *oh*.

'Darren,' I said.

'Yep.'

'It isn't paper.'

'Course it is.'

'It's not. It's money.'

I felt the blood draining from my face. The 'piece of paper' Gamble had spotted was actually a ten-pound note. And it was part of a massive, untidy pile of loads of other notes and coins. There must've been thousands of pounds there, just dumped on the floor. I clutched a massive handful of it and let it fall through my fingers.

'Rubbish,' said Gamble, still sitting up on top of the boxes, 'why would a delivery van be stuffed full of mo–'

He didn't get the chance to finish because the side door of the van suddenly slammed shut.

Everything went pitch black.

We heard the two front doors open.

The van bounced up and down.

The doors closed with a double *thunk*.

'Go! Go! Go!' shouted a man's voice from the front of the van.

The engine spluttered into life.

'Let's get out of here!' screamed a woman.

The tyres screeched. Stones were flung up onto the bottom of the van as it lurched forward.

I was thrown to the floor.

Gamble landed on top of me.

We swerved round a corner.

What on earth was happening?

Roller Coaster

It was impossible to know how fast we were going or in which direction. The van was whining and juddering as though it was alive and in extreme pain, and Gamble and I were flung from side to side, slamming into the walls and each other. Boxes and bottles and who knows what else rained down on us.

Gamble was excited. 'This is well good!' he cried. 'It's like a roller coaster.'

I, on the other hand, was absolutely terrified.

Delivery drivers don't drive like maniacs, I thought. Something was seriously wrong.

'Go faster!' shouted the woman in the front.

'Yeah! Faster, faster!' yelled Gamble.

'We've got to get out of here!' I wailed at Gamble over the howling engine.

'Sure,' said Gamble. I heard him pulling on the back-door handle.

I dragged him away. 'Are you mental? If we hit the road we'll be turned into scrambled eggs.'

The van swung round another bend, knocking us to the floor again.

'We've got to wait till it stops,' I said. 'Then we'll get out and call the police.'

'No way,' he said, 'Gambles don't call the police. I've got a better idea.'

He crawled forward. A moment later I heard him knock on the glass window that separated us from the front of the van. Was he crazy? A curtain was pulled back across the glass and a thick beam of light shone through from the cab.

A face was peering through the window. It was covered with a balaclava so only the eyes and mouth were visible.

Delivery drivers don't wear balaclavas, I thought.

The person's eyes opened wide and the curtain was yanked shut again.

'Stop the van!' called the woman's voice.

We screeched to a stop. I was flung forward and bashed into the partition at the front. Boxes, cans and coins flew into the back of me.

'There's two flipping kids in the back!' screamed the woman.

'What d'you mean?' roared the gruff voice of the driver. 'Didn't you check?'

'Why would I check? I was too busy emptying out the till.'

Delivery drivers definitely *don't empty tills,* I thought.

I could hear a fist slamming down on the steering wheel. 'How many shops do we have to rob before you learn?'

Yep, I thought, *we've been kidnapped by armed robbers. Of course.*

As soon as I realised this, I became extremely calm about the whole thing.

Well, by calm, I mean that I curled up into a ball and cried, 'We're going to die! We're going to die!'

But Gamble really *was* calm. Too calm, in fact. He stood up, pressed his face against the window and tapped on the glass again.

'What are you doing?' I hissed, peeping up from between my fingers. 'Get down!'

Gamble ignored me and knocked again.

Two balaclava-covered faces appeared on the other side of the window.

They stared at Gamble for what felt like hours.

'Darren?' said the driver, suddenly. 'What are you doing here?'

They knew Gamble?

'All right, Uncle Terry?' said Gamble. 'Hiya, Auntie Pat.'

Nope. Even worse. They were related to him.

It felt like my brain was about to burst.

Stuck

The side door of the van was thrown open and I blinked against the bright sunlight. The two robbers had rolled their balaclavas up over their heads. Gamble's uncle looked a lot like a chubby version of Gamble. Laughing, he helped us out of the van.

'Sorry about that, boys,' he said. 'For some reason we were in a bit of a rush.'

This seemed to be hilarious because all three of them burst out laughing.

'What are you doing?' asked Gamble.

His uncle sniffed. 'Oh, you know. Picking up some things to sell on and make a few quid. The usual.'

Yep, that's totally 'usual', I thought.

'Gotta make a living somehow,' he sighed. 'All those creams and tablets aren't cheap.'

'Oh. How *are* your worms?' said Gamble.

'Don't ask,' said his uncle, scratching his backside. 'That van seat's killing me. One lesson I've learned – never let a dog sleep in your bed.'

I shuddered. Gamble's uncle robbed shops so he could afford to cure the worms in his bottom that he'd probably caught from that disgusting dog. Why didn't that surprise me?

'You must be Darren's friend,' said Gamble's auntie, leaning in to me. She was wearing heavy pink lipstick that was smudged across her face from the balaclava and she was missing one of her front teeth. 'Roman, isn't it? He's always on about you, you know.'

Gamble hunched his shoulders, looking totally embarrassed.

'Oh yeah,' said Gamble's uncle. 'We had tea round his mum's last night. It was "Roman this" and "Roman that".'

'We're just glad he's got a good pal,' said Gamble's auntie, ruffling my hair. 'He's the angel of our family, after all.'

'Oh,' I said.

'You didn't do anything to Mr Gibson, did you?' said Gamble. 'He still owes Spud twenty-eight quid.'

His uncle laughed hard. 'Oh no, Darren. You know me – big teddy bear. Made him a cup of tea then locked him in the toilet.'

At that point, we heard a distant police siren. 'Uh-oh. Here come the fuzz,' said Gamble's auntie. 'We'd best be off.'

'You'll understand if we don't give you a lift,' said his uncle, hopping up into the van.

'Course. Mind if we grab some doughnuts?' Gamble said.

His uncle started the van. 'Be quick about it. And make sure you give that shopkeeper some money for 'em.'

'Aye,' said his auntie, 'I won't hear anyone say the Gambles don't pay their way.'

I had no idea what to say about this.

Gamble hopped up into the van, rummaged around a bit and jumped out with both boxes under his arms. I slammed the door behind him.

The police siren was getting louder. 'Tell your Mum we'll see her on Sunday,' said his auntie from the window, 'unless the police catch us. Then it'll be more like next Christmas. Toodle-pip!'

They roared away and disappeared round a tight bend as Gamble stood next to me, calmly waving goodbye.

'Funny seeing them, wasn't it?' he said.

My knees finally gave way and I flopped myself down on the grass verge. 'Your uncle and auntie are armed robbers,' I said.

'No,' said Gamble, 'They're not *armed*. Just robbers, that's all. Big difference.'

'Right,' I said, as though this made everything OK.

At that moment, a police car zoomed past at high speed, its sirens blaring and lights flashing. We jumped back, away from the road.

Gamble sniffed. 'Looks like I won't be seeing 'em again for a while,' he said. For a moment he sounded sad but then he suddenly cheered up. 'Oh well. Still – they quite like it in prison. They get to spend time with the rest of the family.'

After a long silence I decided to change the subject. 'Where are we anyway?'

Gamble pointed to a road sign that said 'Town Centre: 3 miles'.

Perfect. We were in the middle of nowhere. 'Do you still have my mobile?' I asked.

Gamble pulled it out of his pocket and handed it over. 'I meant to give it back but . . . you know . . . habit,' he said.

I looked at my phone. In the last twenty-four hours, Jane had sent me thirty-seven texts. All of them said the same thing:

Remember the doughnuts. Or else.

I decided to ignore her and dialled my home number. The phone beeped three times and a computer voice said: 'Sorry. You do not have enough credit to make this call. Your current balance is *zero* pence.'

Eh? I'd had over three quid before I entered that competition the other night. There must been some mistake. I tried again but the same thing happened.

'Darren, did you use my phone?' I asked.

Gamble gave a cub-scout salute. 'Nope, honest I didn't, I promise you can't prove it.'

I rolled my eyes and we set off walking.

FRIDAY

Part One

The Old People's Tea Party Goes Really Well
and the Deadly Doughnut Finally Stops
Ruining My Life . . . Sort Of

It took me almost an hour to get home. By the time
I walked through the door it was nearly five o'clock.
Mum was pretty annoyed but I told her I'd been
sorting things out for the old people's tea party (which
wasn't too much of a fib) and she calmed down.
Over the evening I had another forty texts from Jane
'reminding' me about the doughnuts; I had no credit,
though, so I couldn't reply. I guess I could've answered
over the internet or something but I didn't really
want to get into a conversation with her.

The next morning I met Gamble on the way to school. He was carrying the Squidgy Splodge boxes, which he'd insisted on looking after, and there was an enormous plastic bag hanging from his wrist. He said it contained the costume for his performance. When I asked if I could see his costume he told me to go away in quite an aggressive manner. At Mr Gibson's shop, he waited outside while I went in to explain about the doughnuts.

I hadn't been looking forward to this but, amazingly, Mr Gibson was in a great mood. After the police had arrested Gamble's auntie and uncle, they'd given him back all the money from his safe and everything else they'd found in the van, even though some of it wasn't his. He was even more chuffed when I told him that Gamble had promised not to bother him again.

At school, we found Jane nervously waiting at the gate. The moment she saw the doughnuts she squealed with delight. 'Oh, Romy! You got them! You're so amazing!'

'Yep,' I replied, pretending not to notice her kissing me on the cheek. 'Well . . . Gamble helped.'

Gamble shrugged his shoulders. ''S what I do.'

The only downer on the whole morning was Mrs

McDonald. When we went inside, she was sitting on the floor by the hole in the skirting board, rocking backwards and forwards. There were red rims around her eyes and she was still wearing yesterday's clothes. 'Here, piggy-wiggy,' she said, like she hadn't noticed us come in. Had she been there all night?

Gamble put his hand on her shoulder. She blinked at him like he was a stranger.

'Miss, I think you should have a rest,' he said softly. 'I'll sit here this morning and wait for Mr Wiggles.'

Mrs McDonald didn't answer for a few seconds. 'But I can't . . . I . . .'

Gamble helped Mrs McDonald to her feet and over to her desk. 'I'll do it, miss, cos I love you, miss,' said Gamble.

'We can make welcome posters for the old people while you rest,' suggested Jane.

'And I'll put some doughnut out for him, miss,' said Gamble as Miss Clegg strolled in late.

'Oh, Darren. You're so sweet,' said Mrs McDonald. 'I'm sorry for all the times I've been strict with you.'

'Huh, he's probably poisoned it,' muttered Miss Clegg.

I thought this was pretty harsh. I mean, Gamble was trying his best to be kind.

'Shut your gob, you crusty turnip bum,' said Gamble, no longer trying his best to be kind.

For the first time ever, Miss Clegg looked wide awake. 'Did you hear the way he spoke to me?'

Mrs McDonald flopped down on her chair. 'Didn't hear a thing,' she said.

I could swear that, as she rested her head on her desk, she gave Gamble a little wink.

You Can Trust Me

The old people were going to arrive at eleven o'clock. Rosie, Jane and I spent playtime in the hall, setting out tables and chairs, sticking up the posters everyone had made in class, and putting paper napkins onto plates. Meanwhile Miss Clegg, who was still in a terrible mood, made a huge urn of tea and put the doughnuts from one of the boxes out onto a plate. We'd left the other box in the store cupboard in the classroom where it's dark and cool. I was desperate to eat one but Jane told me there'd be plenty of time for that later. 'Don't worry, Romy,' she said, 'I won't let our four-day anniversary pass without you having a doughnut.'

This was good enough for me. She seemed back to her old self now so I didn't want to cause any arguments.

'When the old people are here, I'll take photos and Jane will serve the doughnuts,' announced Rosie, tying her hair back in a ponytail. 'Roman, you'll go back to the classroom when we need more supplies, but keep out of the way the rest of the time.'

'Why can't I serve the old people?' I asked.

'Because you're a hideous ugly freak,' Rosie said, smiling.

'Thanks a bunch,' I said.

After break, we went back to class. Mrs McDonald was sitting by the hole in the wall again, holding a piece of doughnut and making *kiss-kiss* noises.

Meanwhile, Gamble was getting changed in the cupboard at the back of the room. He refused to come out till we'd all gone because he didn't want us to see his costume. Miss Clegg told him he had three seconds to get out but Mrs McDonald told her that Darren had earned the right to some privacy. Miss Clegg muttered something about locking the door and throwing away the key.

Mr Noblet came into the room. 'OK, guys, the seniors have arrived. Time to shine!'

We lined up at the door but Mrs McDonald stayed where she was.

'Ahem,' said Mr Noblet. 'Mrs McDonald, I know that finding your guinea pig is important but we *really* need you out there to look after your class.'

Mrs McDonald stood up. 'I will not leave this hole. What if Mr Wiggles turns up while I'm out?'

'I'll stay,' said Rosie Taylor, stepping out of the line.

'You've got jobs in the hall,' said Jane.

'You'll manage,' said Rosie.

Mr Noblet looked doubtful. 'We're not meant to leave pupils on their own . . .'

'It's her or me,' snapped Mrs McDonald.

'You'll only be next door,' simpered Rosie. 'You can trust me.'

I didn't like the way she smiled; she looked like a seagull just before it nicks your chips.

This made me feel uncomfortable but I didn't have time to say anything. As soon as we'd tucked our shirts in and flattened our hair, we went straight out to reception to meet the old people. Their bus was parked outside, right in front of the main entrance.

It had 'Winter Sun Retirement Village' written on the side of it. A couple of cheerful carers helped the old people off the bus and each of us had to bring one of them through to the hall.

I'd guess that their average age was around eighty-five. A few of them were using wheelchairs or zimmer frames. They were a jolly bunch and they seemed delighted to be out for the day.

I was helping a lively old gentleman called Bernard who told me he was ninety-six! I had to wait for him to be lowered off the back of the bus on his electric mobility scooter. He had a handlebar moustache and a row of medals on his blazer. He kept telling me he'd lost his glasses, which might've been why he said: 'Thank you, my dear girl,' when I opened the door for him then, as he scooted through, winked at me and said, 'By gum, you nurses are getting younger and prettier all the time.'

We led the old people into the hall and sat them down. Bernard left his scooter by the wall-bars and walked over to a chair using a stick. 'Don't really need the scooter,' he said mischievously. 'I just use it for impressing the ladies.'

Well, I thought, *it's not exactly an open-top Porsche but still . . .*

We'd set out the tables in a horseshoe so everyone was facing the stage. As the old people settled down, Mr Noblet stood up and made a speech to say welcome and, 'wasn't it nice that some of the Year Sixes had organised this and blah . . . blah . . . blah . . . talented musicians to perform and blah . . . blah . . . let's serve the tea and cakes!'

Everyone cheered and applauded the last bit.

When the clapping had died down, Bernard turned to me and said: 'Who on earth was that funny-looking woman?'

I sniggered. For the first time in a while I actually felt happy. I wasn't worrying about doughnuts or guinea pigs or girlfriends and, very soon, I was going to finally tuck into a delicious jam doughnut of my own. It had been a long and difficult week, but things were finally looking up!

Miss Clegg and Jane brought round cups of tea and doughnuts while the old people happily chatted away about their lives. On one table, I could see Kevin 'The Vomcano' Harrison with a doughnut in each hand, sort-of listening to an old lady.

'I was in the army you know: 1940, Battle of Dunkirk,' said Bernard, half to me and half to no one at all. 'Trapped by the enemy. Sniper's rifle shoved under my nose. I looked right down the barrel and I said . . . Ooh lovely, my favourite.'

At first, I thought that this was the strangest war story of all time. But then I realised that Jane was holding the plate of doughnuts out in front of us. I reached out and she knocked my hand away. 'Old people first, Roman,' she said, as Bernard took the last two.

'I'll have to get some more,' said Jane. She curtseyed and apologised to the other old people on the table, who narrowed their eyes at Bernard.

Bernard didn't seem to care, though. He held the doughnuts one on top of another like a big cakey skyscraper. Then, as I licked my lips at the sight of them, he removed his false teeth and stuffed both doughnuts into his mouth at once.

'Nese are nood nonuts,' he said, chunks of dough spraying out everywhere.

I shuddered. At that moment, Jane tapped me on the shoulder. 'Roman, we're all out of doughnuts. The old folk have eaten the first box.'

'Already?'

'They're absolutely guzzling them,' she said. 'I've not even had one yet. You'll have to go back to the classroom and get some more.'

Some of the old people on my table were becoming restless. 'Are there any more of those doughnuts?' said one old lady as I stood up.

'That table've got doughnuts. Why haven't we?' grumbled another pensioner.

'You keep quiet, Agnes. It's our turn first,' hissed a woman on the next table.

I stood up and edged away. An old man gripped my wrist tightly as I walked past him. 'Doughnuts!' he growled threateningly.

I eased his fingers off but other old people were shuffling out of their places towards me. Mr Noblet was chatting to a bunch of old women who – yuck! – seemed to be *flirting* with him. Miss Clegg was busy with the tea, and Mrs McDonald was sitting on her own, looking a little dazed.

'Distract them with some music,' I said to Jane, urgently. 'I'll go and get the box.'

I was out of breath when I reached the classroom. It was empty. Gamble must've gone round the outside of school to get to the hall. Wow! He really was desperate for this costume to be a surprise.

There was no sign of Rosie either. Typical. She'd promised Mrs McDonald she'd wait here to look out for Mr Wiggles then she'd just wandered off somewhere. I knew she couldn't be trusted! There wasn't time to waste worrying about Rosie, though. I weaved my way through the tables towards the store cupboard.

And that's when I saw it.

Right in front of the cupboard door was a beautiful jam doughnut. It was sitting on top of a piece of paper with a printed message on it that read:

```
To My Boyfriend Roman.
Go on, you deserve it!
  Love Jane xxxx
```

Good grief!

She must've nipped in here when I wasn't looking then sent me on this errand as a special treat. Wow! An anniversary present! She'd said she wouldn't let the day go past without me eating a doughnut and here it was! What a lovely thing to do. I knew I was in a rush but still . . . how long had it been since my last doughnut? Well, if I wanted to be precise: four days, seventeen hours and eleven minutes.

The old people could wait a few more moments, couldn't they?

I dived forward and grabbed the doughnut with

both hands. Then I opened my mouth wide and stuffed as much as I could fit inside it. There was one incredible moment when the taste hit my tongue and then . . .

The cupboard door flew open. There was a flash of light.

'Gotcha!' cried Rosie Taylor.

You've No Idea What You Did

'What are you doing?' I asked, swallowing.

Rosie put the school camera into her pocket. 'Gathering evidence,' she said, quickly grabbing up the note off the floor. 'You've been papped. And you're gonna be in big trouble.'

'But . . . but . . .' I stammered.

Gamble's clothes were strewn across the floor of the cupboard. Rosie kicked them out of the way and stepped over to the shredding machine, which was sitting on a shelf. She carefully fed the note from Jane into it. The blades whirred and the machine chewed it up.

Wait a minute. There was something on the blades of the shredding machine.

'Is that . . . *jam?*' I said.

Rosie smiled smugly. 'Yes, Roman. While you've been out there, I've been very busy indeed.'

Very slowly I realised something. Oh no! Surely not . . .

'Hang on. Have you been . . . *shredding* the doughnuts?'

She reached down, picked up the doughnut box from the shelf and turned it upside down. A few granules of sugar floated to the ground. 'Yes!' she said, laughing like a cartoon super-villain. 'Every single one of them.'

I took a step backwards. 'I don't want to be horrible,' I said, 'but are you mental? Normal people don't shred delicious cakes, Rosie.'

'But I *hate* doughnuts, Roman,' she said, flinging the box to one side and jabbing me in the chest with her finger. 'And I hate you. And you're finally going to get what you deserve for all the misery you've caused me.'

'"What I deserve"?' I asked, totally confused. 'What do you mean? Are you setting me up?'

Rosie laughed like a maniac. 'I've waited so long for this. It's the perfect plan. I've got photographic evidence to prove that you stole doughnuts from the mouths of old people. You'll be in mega-trouble.

Everyone will hate you.' She clicked her fingers and waved her hand in front of my face. 'Hashtag: *shameful.*'

'But . . . I don't understand. What are you doing? Why do you hate me so much? I thought . . . I thought . . . we used to be friends.'

'Friends? Pah,' she said, practically spitting the words out at me. 'You've no idea what you did to me, have you?'

Confused, I shook my head.

Rosie ran her finger along the top of the shredder. 'When we were younger we used to play together all the time. In fact, when we were four our favourite game was pretending to marry each other.'

'Well. That *was* a long time ago,' I said.

'You're telling me,' she said, bitterly. 'Our mums thought it was "cute".' Rosie did that annoying speech marks thing that people do with their fingers. 'Then one day you did something truly awful.'

'Look,' I said, 'I've got to get back. I don't know why you're . . .'

Rosie glared at me so aggressively that I stopped mid-sentence. 'I was at your house,' she said after a moment. 'We were acting out one of our pretend weddings, and I was wearing my brand-new birthday present: a sparkly Cinderella dress. It was perfect.'

I glanced over towards the door. 'That's great but I *need* to go . . .'

'Shut up, Roman!' she snapped. 'Of course, I looked fabulous – my beautiful hair cascading down my back, the sequins on my dress twinkling – but as usual you hadn't bothered to make an effort. You were dressed as Postman Pat.'

She spat the last two words out at me. 'He was my favourite,' I said lamely.

Rosie ignored me. 'Just as I was making you promise to love me and obey me forever and ever Amen, your mum called up that it was snack-time, and there were doughnuts downstairs. Without so much as an *I do,* you sprinted off and left me there. On my wedding day! I was *crushed.*'

There was a few moments' silence.

'Is that it?' I said. 'I mean, I'm sorry but it *was* only a game.'

'NO, THAT'S NOT IT!' she shrieked so loudly that I took a step backwards. 'Don't you remember what happened next?'

'I was only little.'

'Well, I'll never forget it.' She narrowed her eyes.

'I'd promised my mum I'd keep my princess dress clean so I decided to take it off before following you downstairs. I got it up over my head but I'd been wearing the dress over my other clothes and it was quite tight. Before I knew it I was stuck. The dress was covering my face and I couldn't move my arms. I needed someone to help me out of it but my "husband" had gone.'

It took me a moment to realise she meant me. 'Oh. Sorry about that.'

Rosie ignored me. 'I couldn't see where I was going, so I couldn't get downstairs. I called and called but nobody came. So there I was, alone and trapped. I wriggled one arm round to try and loosen the zip and then –' she took a deep breath and stared straight into my eyes – 'the zip got caught in my hair.'

'I still don't s–'

'Shut it, Roman!' she hissed. 'I was blinded and stuck with this huge puffy dress over my head. The more I pulled at the zip, the more knotted my hair became. I felt like my whole scalp was being pulled off and I could barely breathe! I screamed and struggled for ages, but by the time your mum finally came to find me I'd almost passed out. She tried

to help me but my hair was completely tangled . . .
so she had to . . . to . . . ' Rosie paused, clearly
distressed. 'She had to cut a massive clump of it
out. My princess hair, Roman!'

Rosie reached into her pocket and pulled out a
crumpled photo. '*This* is what I looked like!' The
picture was of a young and chubby Rosie scowling
at the camera. The whole front part of her hair
was missing. She looked scary yet ridiculous at the
same time, like a really angry coconut.

'Have you any idea how humiliating this hairstyle
was for a child as fabulous as me?' she snarled.

'Well . . . er . . . you *were* only four,' I said. I
guess maybe this explains why she messes about
with her hair all the time.

'Age isn't important, Roman – I was traumatised!
I had to wear a hat for three months. I've kept that
photo with me ever since; it's been my reminder
that one day I had to get my own back on you.'

'But I don't get it. Why shred the old people's
doughnuts?' I asked, more confused than ever.

'After your mother had hacked off half my hair,
she tried to make me feel better. I was crying, and
she said a jam doughnut might cheer me up. Like
a fool, I believed her. But when I got downstairs

to the kitchen, my plate was empty. You'd gobbled up yours then helped yourself to mine as well!'

'Ah,' I said. 'I probably thought you didn't want it . . .'

Rosie shook her head. 'I'll never forget the way you grinned at me, jam smeared around your greedy little cheeks. You are a heartless, nasty little turd, Roman Garstang: all you care about is food. You chose a doughnut over our friendship, our wedding, my happiness *and* my hair!'

I gulped.

'I've hated you from that moment on,' continued Rosie, her voice now a sinister whisper. She untied her ponytail and shook her hair loose. 'Every day I've had to watch you at school, scoffing doughnuts and rubbing my face in it. I've been waiting all this time for my chance to make you pay. And now, finally, it's arrived.'

So this was why she'd always hated me.

'But, I didn't mean to,' I said. 'I just . . . really like doughnuts. I'm sorry.'

'Too late,' she said.

Maybe there was a way to save myself. 'Surely the shredding machine is full of doughnuts?' I said.

'Already emptied and cleaned,' she said smugly.

'A quick wipe of the blades and there won't be a trace of them left.'

I glanced over at the shredding machine on the shelf. This was my only chance. I had to prevent her from wiping it clean. I lunged forward.

Rosie did too, but she suddenly went flying, flipping the shredder off the shelf with her outstretched hand. As she fell, the shredder landed on the top of her head with a loud '*donk*' and bounced onto the floor.

Rosie ended up sitting under the shelf, her back propped up against the wall. Gamble's trousers were tangled around her ankles. She must've tripped over them.

Crikey, I thought, *I* knew *trousers were dangerous* . . .

'Rosie. Are you OK?' I asked.

She stared at me with glassy eyes, her head wobbling about. 'Oh, I'm fine. Really fine. Think I'll have a little snooze . . .'

And with that, she slumped sideways onto the floor and fell fast asleep.

As quickly as I could, I checked the back of her head to see if she was injured. Her hair was wet with something red. *Yikes!* I dabbed gingerly at it

with my hand. It felt a bit too sticky to be blood
and it looked like there might be crumbs in it . . .
Nervously I licked my fingers. *Phew!* It was jam
from the blades of the shredding machine.

'I'm going to get help. Don't go anywhere!' I said,
before realising how stupid this sounded.

Rosie snored back at me.

I sprinted back through the school. The reception
desk was empty so I ran straight into the hall.

Pandemonium

The old people's tea party was pandemonium. I
tried to get to Mr Noblet but he was trapped in
the corner, surrounded by pensioners demanding
food. The rest of the old people were bashing their
fists on the tables chanting: 'DOUGH-NUT!
DOUGH-NUT! DOUGH-NUT!'

I looked around. Mrs McDonald was sitting
glumly behind the tea urn. I ran over to her. 'Mrs
McDonald, it's Rosie. Quick,' I said but she didn't
seem to hear me. She just sat there muttering to
herself: 'He's never coming back. He's never coming
back.' On stage, Jane was speaking nervously into
the microphone. 'Now, please. The doughnuts *are*

coming soon. If you'd like to return to your seats we're going to have some live music.'

Kevin 'The Vomcano' Harrison stepped onto the stage holding his trumpet.

'Get off!' cried an old woman.

'We want doughnuts!' shouted a man.

Kevin looked terrified. 'I don't think I can do this,' he said, clutching his stomach and sprinting off stage to loud boos.

Jane looked around her and mouthed 'Help!' to me. There was nothing *I* could do, though. I needed an adult to check on Rosie, and I needed them quickly. Panicking, I looked around for Miss Clegg. She was over by the stereo, cueing up a CD. I tried to run towards her but several old people blocked my path, holding their empty plates up at me. 'Doughnut . . . doughnut . . .' they moaned. It was like being in a zombie movie.

Then Gamble stepped onto the stage.

He was dressed as a lamb. *A lamb*. Honestly. I've never seen anything like it! He was wearing a fluffy white suit, and a little hat with floppy ears that covered his baked bean head. If I didn't know him, I'd have said he looked innocent. Some people might even have described him as 'cute'.

One or two of the old people noticed him. 'Ooooh, isn't he adorable?' said one old lady. The tension in the room seemed to seep away as the pensioners all nudged each other and said 'awwww'. A few people drifted back to their seats.

I could reach Mr Noblet now. I set off just as Gamble took the microphone. He waited for his backing CD to start. There was a mellow introduction of violins, then he began to sing.

'Baa, baa, black sheep, have you any wool?' he sang, his voice even softer and more delicate than it had been the day before. It was so beautiful that I stopped, almost forgetting about Rosie for a moment.

After the first verse the music paused and so did Gamble, his eyes closed.

'What a fine young man,' said Bernard over the silence.

'Like an angel,' cooed an old lady.

Not quite, I thought, but at least everyone had calmed down. Now all he had to do was keep on singing and maybe I could get some help for Rosie.

But Gamble remained still and silent on stage. Nothing happened.

The crowd began to shuffle about.

'Is that it?' asked an old lady.

Nope. Unfortunately, that wasn't it,

Gamble's Performance

Suddenly there was a howl of guitars and a smashing of drums from the stereo. Gamble ripped open the front of his white fluffy lamb costume. To my horror, fake intestines poured out onto the stage. 'NO, YOU CAN'T HAVE SOME WOOL COS I'M TOTALLY CRAZY!!!!!!!!!' he screamed, spraying what I hope was tomato ketchup out of the wound in the front of his outfit.

The room was frozen. Gamble began leaping round the stage, roaring into the microphone: 'I'M A MEAN PSYCHO SHEEP AND I'M GONNA EAT YOUR BRAI-EEE-AIIINS!!!!!!!!!' while the deafening music blasted out of the stereo.

Then he stood on the end of the stage, waggling his tongue about and spraying tomato ketchup into the faces of the pensioners on the front row. Some of them were holding their hands up to their hearts. Others were ripping their hearing aids out of their ears. Miss Clegg was frantically trying to turn off the stereo but nothing could stop Gamble. Even when the music finally stopped he screeched into the microphone one last time before diving off the stage and crashing into a table, sending tea flying everywhere.

There was a long, terrible silence.

'Good heavens,' boomed Bernard, who was standing on the stage, holding a wire with a plug dangling from it, 'who organised this thing?'

I looked around for Jane but she was nowhere to be seen. Mr Noblet looked as surprised and horrified as anyone else. Miss Clegg was pretending to fiddle with the CD player and Mrs McDonald hadn't moved from behind the tea urn. For some reason, Bernard's eyes met mine.

'Ah,' I said, 'Well . . .'

I probably shouldn't have said anything at all. If I'd kept my mouth shut, the old people might've blamed someone else. Instead, they all turned on me. I felt like a lightning rod for the whole room's anger.

'You exploded my hearing aid!' cried one old woman.

'I nearly had a heart attack,' moaned an old man.

'You promised us doughnuts, and you didn't deliver!' said someone else.

'Get her!' yelled Bernard, hobbling across the stage. It took me a moment to realise he meant *me*.

The old people murmured in agreement and slowly began limping towards me, false teeth bared, walking sticks waving angrily in the air, zimmer frames rattling like war chariots.

'Now now,' said Mr Noblet, 'let's not do anything hasty . . .'

But the old people ignored him. I backed away towards the corner of the room but I had no escape route. I was surrounded. They were getting closer. I cowered against the wall-bars and then . . .

'Jump on!' cried Gamble, gliding to a stop between me and the advancing army of pensioners.

'What are you doing?' I yelled. He was sitting on Bernard's electric mobility scooter, still dressed as a butchered lamb.

Without answering, he shot the mobility scooter forward, knocking my legs from under me. I suddenly found my backside stuck fast in the shopping basket.

'Hey! That's mine, you ragamuffins!' yelled Bernard.

But Gamble didn't care. With me firmly wedged into the basket like a massive shopping bag, we skimmed across the room at about three miles per hour. The old people hobbled behind us, blocking the teachers' path. My feet were the battering ram to open the double doors to the hall and before I knew it we were in the school foyer.

'Somebody check on Rosi*eeeeee* . . .' I shouted behind me as we left but nobody seemed to hear me.

We headed straight for the front doors of the school. Just in time, I managed to kick out at the green button that opens them and we trundled through, out into the car park.

'What are we doing?' I said to Gamble.

'Simple,' he replied, bent forward over the handlebars, holding the scooter at full throttle. 'Ferry to France, then down through Spain into Africa, grow some beards and work in Morocco as rug salesmen.'

I had to admit that this was quite a well thought-out plan. Complete rubbish, but well thought-out anyway. 'Darren,' I said, 'we're going slower than walking pace. We'll be fifty years old by the time we get there. Just stop the scooter and let me off.'

Gamble grabbed my shoulder and pinned me down. 'No way, buddy. You're going nowhere.'

At that moment, a lorry swung round into the car park.

'Watch out!' I screamed.

Gamble twisted the handlebars to one side, bumping into a kerb and tipping the scooter into a hedge.

'Awesome!' he said.

Face down in the bush, my buttocks still jammed into the shopping basket, I didn't agree with him at all.

Within moments, and led by Mr Noblet and Mrs McDonald, the angry mob of senior citizens surrounded us again.

'I should hope you're going to give these hooligans a jolly good thrashing,' said Bernard, his moustache flapping up and down like a hyperactive ferret.

'Brutalise the little worms,' snapped an old woman, jabbing at my ribs with her walking stick.

Just then the doors of the lorry swung open. A lady in a posh-looking trouser suit and high heels lowered herself out of the passenger side and tottered over. 'I'm looking for a Darren Gamble,' she said, flashing a mouthful of brilliant white teeth.

Gamble ran forward. 'Me, me, me, me!'

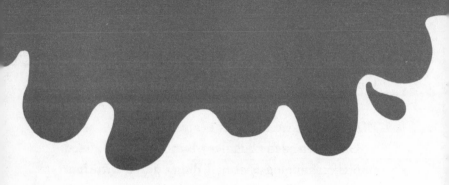

Part Two

The Deadly Doughnut Finally Pays Off

'My name's Angela, and I'm from the Squidgy Splodge Doughnut Company,' she began, 'Congratulations, Darren, you are our winner of the week!'

From inside the bush, I watched as she took a single party popper out of her pocket and let it off, before pulling out a camera and snapping away at Gamble, who was still dressed as a half-mutilated sheep. He gave a series of strongman poses for the camera, grinning and flexing his scrawny muscles.

'So,' she said to Gamble. 'Where should we put your year's supply of doughnuts?'

'Doughnuts?' I said, struggling out of the basket and onto my feet. 'What? Who? How?'

Angela put her hand on Gamble's shoulder. 'Darren's text really was beautiful.'

Gamble smiled proudly.

She pulled a piece of paper out of her pocket and read: 'I want to win this competition so I can help my teacher get her guinea pig back cos she is well beautiful and I love her. Also I want to give some to my best friend in the whole world Roman cos he loves me even though everyone thinks I'm a wrong un and I've borrowed his phone to write this even though he doesn't know about it.' She wiped a tear from her eye and said, 'Strictly speaking it's three texts but still . . . beautiful. Really captures the power of a Squidgy Splodge doughnut.'

'Did you really say that?' I asked Darren.

'I used your phone when I nicked it the other day,' he said, looking at his shoes. 'Thought I should say something about you, innit.'

I cleared my throat. 'That's really . . . ahem . . . *kind* of you . . . er . . . *mate*.'

His smile nearly burst the sides of his face. 'Mate! Did you hear that everyone? Me and Roman are best mates forever.'

'All right. No need to shout about it,' I said, looking over my shoulder to see who could hear him.

At the back of the lorry, the driver was unloading a whole stack of boxes. 'Where do you want these?' he said gruffly.

'Give 'em to my best mate Roman,' beamed Darren.

I looked at him, my mouth hanging open. 'What, all of them?'

He shrugged. 'Well, Mrs McDonald can have a couple to get her guinea pig back. I'm not that into doughnuts. The last one I ate had dog slobber on it. Put me off a bit.'

I ran to the boxes. 'This is unbelievable!' I cried. 'Amazing. Incredible. Thank you so much, Darren! This is the greatest thing that's ever . . . *hang on a minute*.'

I felt my heart sink as I read the writing on the boxes aloud: '"Lemon Curd". But I *hate* lemon-flavoured ones.'

'Beggars can't be choosers,' sniffed the lorry driver.

I felt like I was about to cry. This was like winning a sports car then finding out it was actually a *model* of a sports car carved out of ear-wax. 'Nooooooo!' I cried.

Mr Noblet coughed. 'Might I . . . er . . . suggest

'. . . that if Darren and Roman shared a few of these . . . we could all forgive and forget and go back to our tea party?'

'First sensible thing you've said all day, old girl,' said Bernard.

I stroked my hand down the pile of boxes and grimly nodded my head. 'We might as well,' I sighed.

Back inside the hall, the old people were soon happy again. The doughnuts were flowing fast and disaster had been avoided. I watched everyone else tucking in, trying not to be too disappointed.

Jane came over to me. She was holding a plate with six doughnuts on it. 'Romy,' she said, 'I've been thinking. Maybe we should just be friends. I'm a bit young to have a boyfriend. And anyway, I'm not really sure if it was you I liked or your doughnuts.'

I shrugged. To be honest, I wasn't bothered at all. I was so numb about the lemon doughnuts that everything else seemed completely pointless.

'You wouldn't mind if I took a few more doughnuts home with me, would you? You know, as a "breaking-up" present.'

I shrugged again.

'Thanks, Romy,' she said, before skipping off.

Once she'd gone, Kevin 'The Vomcano' Harrison

appeared, his cheeks stuffed with doughnut. 'This is brilliant!' he said. 'I've already had eight and I don't feel sick at all!'

'Lovely,' I said, taking a step back, just in case.

The only person who didn't look happy was Mrs McDonald, who was sitting on her own.

Suddenly, there was a piercing scream from somewhere in the school. It sounded like . . .

'Rosie Taylor!' I yelled. In the kerfuffle, and the surprise of the doughnut delivery, I'd forgotten all about her. I felt awful.

Mrs McDonald sprang to her feet. 'Was that coming from our room?' she said.

The scream came again, louder than before.

We all sprinted back to the classroom. When we got there, we found Rosie Taylor still lying face down on the floor of the cupboard. She appeared to be hyperventilating. 'Get them off me! Get them off me!' she panted.

'What's wrong with you?' said Mrs McDonald.

The words tumbled desperately out of Rosie's mouth. 'Just get them off me NOW!'

Mrs McDonald put her hand to her mouth. Then she suddenly dived forward and grabbed something off Rosie's face. 'My darling! I've found you!'

Mr Wiggles!

Rosie remained frozen to the ground, crying out: 'They're still on me! They're still on me!'

'What are you talking about, child?' said Mrs McDonald, clutching Mr Wiggles to her chest. Then her face dropped. 'Good grief. Your hair is moving!'

I peered into the dim cupboard and I couldn't believe my eyes. Crawling through Rosie's hair and across her face were four tiny, wriggling furballs.

'Please help me!' she sobbed, as one of the furballs crawled across her ear.

Mrs McDonald turned on the light. 'Holy piggy-wiggy!' she said. 'They can't be . . . but they look like . . . yes they are! Baby guinea pigs!'

'Aaaargh!' screamed Rosie. 'That's disgusting! The rat gave birth in my hair! My beautiful princess hair! Ruined again!'

'Oh, be quiet, you silly girl,' said Mrs McDonald, carefully scooping up the baby guinea pigs and carrying them over to the cage. 'They won't have been born in your hair. Mr Wiggles and the babies were probably nice and cosy somewhere till you came along. It's your fault for lying down with jam all over your head. No wonder they crawled onto you.'

Rosie scrabbled at her face and hair, panting, 'Yuck-yuck-yuck-yuck.'

I took this opportunity to pick the camera up off the floor and delete the photo of me eating the doughnut, just in case.

'You weren't fat after all,' gushed Mrs McDonald to her bald guinea pig, nuzzling its nose before placing it into the cage with its babies. 'You were pregnant all along, my clever Mr Wiggles. Or should I call you *Mrs* Wiggles?'

Rosie stood up, practically crying. 'O-M-G!' she exclaimed. 'Hashtag: *nothing* could ever be more disgusting than *that*.'

She was wrong about this, though. At that exact moment, Kevin 'The Vomcano' Harrison started deep-breathing. He was standing right in front of Rosie.

'Urgh. Those horrible little creatures were in your hair. I don't like 'em,' he said. 'They're making the doughnuts in my tummy flip about.'

'No,' said Rosie.

Kevin's cheeks puffed out. 'I think I'm going to . . .'

'Get him away from me!' Rosie cried.

But it was too late.

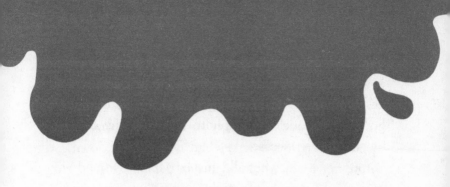

Epilogue

So that was that.

If I hadn't tried to eat that single deadly doughnut at the aquarium, I wouldn't have had to put up with a seriously bossy girlfriend, or have been stung by a jellyfish, bitten by a bald guinea pig, tricked into shoplifting, kidnapped by robbers or very nearly getting framed for stealing from the mouths of hungry senior citizens.

And I guess if I hadn't been so distracted by doughnuts when Rosie was at my house all those years ago, she probably wouldn't have got stuck inside her princess costume and had to have all her hair cut off, and had a vendetta against me ever since . . .

So it's true – doughnuts *are* pretty dangerous.

But then again, it hadn't been all bad. I mean, if it wasn't for the doughnut, I wouldn't have a new best mate (even if he is crazy) *and* I wouldn't have got to see Rosie Taylor get so completely soaked in puke that the caretaker had to hose her down before her mum would let her in the car.

I suppose that maybe they're worth the risk.

In any case, I soon forgot all about the trauma of that school week when I got home on Friday afternoon. Mum had been to the supermarket and bought a great big tray of Squidgy Splodge. Raspberry-flavoured. I ate four before I'd even sat down. And nothing bad has happened to me since.

Well, not yet anyway . . .

Find out what happens to Roman next in

THE Chicken Nugget AMBUSH

On a class trip to Farm View outdoors centre, Roman finds himself not only BANNED from eating doughnuts — !! — but on a strict chicken-nugget-only diet. Eating these little breadcrumbed, ear-shaped snacks three times a day might sound like fun to *you*, but the poultry pieces soon drive Roman to distraction, deadly hunger and total desperation.

He's going to need all the survival skills he can learn to live through. . .

THE CHICKEN NUGGET AMBUSH!

Thank you for choosing a Piccadilly Press book.

If you would like to know more about our
authors, our books or if you'd just like to know
what we're up to, you can find us online.

www.piccadillypress.co.uk

You can also find us on:

We hope to see you soon!